THRIVE IN THE
COMPETITIVE WO...

與國際接軌必備的

中-英

莊琬君 ◎著

展場口譯

展場口譯史上——四大強

- **成效性強：**能靈活應對各展場口譯狀況，展現出駕馭語言使用的能力，口譯證照張張入手。
- **學習性強：**循序漸進學口譯，組織出各種表達句型，在最短時間內將口譯能力最大化。
- **即戰力強：**與時俱進且不斷地學習最新的知識，符合雇主期待，成為各大大小小公司爭相邀聘的譯者。
- **實務性強：**用「行動的實踐」學習必備五大類展場專業分類話題，建立良好品牌形象、打開市場通路和爭取產品訂單，立即成為業主的最佳幫手。

MP3

搞定展場口譯，畢業即就業
累積轉職談判籌碼，策略性包裝，成為耀眼的業界搶手貨

作者序
PREFACE

首先感謝貴社的韋佑編輯及團隊，在筆者撰寫過程中耐心地引導及給予建議。

俗語説：「學習一個新的語言就能打開一個全新的世界」。而歐洲中世紀早期的查理曼大帝曾説：「擁有另一種語言即擁有第二個靈魂」。翻譯的過程，不只牽涉詞彙和文法句型的轉換，也常常需要考慮文化、邏輯、情境等差異。此書除了主題式的單字與翻譯練習，協助讀者打下基本功，也透過包羅萬象的展覽話題，營造各式情境，協助讀者建立背景知識並體會翻譯是全面性的思維轉換，就好像在兩個世界間流轉。

寫作過程中，筆者不自覺地想起英國客體關係理論大師溫尼考特（D. W. Winnicott）提出的潛能空間（potential space）觀念。每個單元都是不同的潛能空間，邀請讀者進入這空間，不只加強英語力，也加強翻譯力。

莊琬君 敬上

編者序
EDITOR

　　口譯一直是門博大精深的領域，求學期間總不乏有許多人想從事口、筆譯工作，而學校課堂大多是理論式的教法。其實除了課堂學習外，口、筆譯最終其實還是要回歸到個人的投入、努力和練習上，不斷地強化自身的表達能力和累積實務經驗，而非僅僅靠學歷光環。書中提供了五大類別的**展場口譯**，讀者能夠在這些基礎類別上再拓展或延伸式的學習相關的類別。

　　書籍除了適合英語系學生在大學時就打好口語跟口譯基礎外，也很適合非英語系學生充實自己，為自己未來求職等做好更多的準備，讓自己比同科系的同學更有競爭優勢。畢竟，隨著市場急遽變化和求職日益嚴峻，比起是否有雙主修和輔系等規劃，雇主仍看重求職者的外語和電腦能力。在履歷表的呈現上，能呈現出自己與其他求職者有明顯地區隔者，往往能雀屏中選。此外，書籍也很適合**英語系授課老師**，在大一、大二的口說課或聽力課當課堂教材，讓學生具備「即戰力」和「競爭力」。最後要感謝作者莊琬君在暢銷書**《iBT新托福寫作書》**後與公司合作了這本具**即效性**和**實務性**極強的口譯書，兩本都堪稱是 **best of the bunch**，誠摯向您推薦這兩本書。

編輯部 敬上

使用說明

34　飯店、餐飲展
國際烘培展
International Bakery Show

口譯專業字彙　基礎字彙

字彙	音標	詞性	中譯
anticipate	[æn`tɪsə‚pet]	v.	期望
triennial	[traɪ`ɛnɪəl]	adj.	三年一次的
announce	[ə`naʊns]		宣布
announcement	[ə`naʊnsmənt]		宣布
historic	[hɪs`tɔrɪk]	adj.	有歷史意義的
hands-on	[`hændz`ɑn]	adj.	實際動手做的
session	[`sɛʃən]	n.	講習會
artisan	[`ɑrtəzn]		工匠、達人
ingredient	[ɪn`gridɪənt]		原料
pastry	[`pestrɪ]		酥皮點心
confectionery	[kən`fɛkʃən‚ɛrɪ]		甜食
acclaimed	[ə`klemd]	adj.	受到讚揚的
logistics	[lo`dʒɪstɪks]		物流
sector	[`sɛktə]		部分、部門
facet	[`fæsɪt]	n.	方面
chef	[ʃɛf]	n.	主廚

220

於口譯演練前熟悉基礎和進階字彙，掌握各展覽主題字彙在實際口譯時，不會因不熟悉字彙而影響表現。

PART 4 · 飯店、餐飲展 34 — 國際烘培展
International Bakery Show

口譯專業字彙　進階字彙

字彙	音標	詞性	中譯
sugarcraft	[`ʃugə‚kræft]	n.	塑糖工藝
fondant	[`fɑndənt]	n.	翻糖
piping	[`paɪpɪŋ]	n.	（蛋糕的）花飾
culinary	[`kjulɪ‚nɛrɪ]	adj.	烹飪的
extruder	[ɛk`strud]		擠出
extruder	[ɛk`strudə]		擠壓機
icing	[`aɪsɪŋ]	n.	糖衣
frosting	[`frɔstɪŋ]		糖霜
curdle	[`kɝd!]	v.	凝結
dredge	[drɛdʒ]	v.	撒粉
sieve	[sɪv]	n.、v.	篩、篩子
knead	[nid]	v.	揉捏
dough	[do]	v.	麵糰
spatula	[`spætjələ]	n.	鏟刀
colander	[`kʌləndə]		濾盆
grater	[`gretə]		磨碎器

221

字彙表更適合教師用於每堂課中抽考或學生自行演練使用。

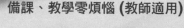

A press conference on the International Bakery Show is being held.

Welcome to the highly-anticipated triennial bakery show. This year we are proud to announce that the number of our exhibitors has reached a historic high, with 665 exhibitors from 52 countries. Another exciting announcement is the new educational section, where artisan bakers will present the latest baking techniques, and hands-on sessions will be provided. Take cake decorating techniques for example, they feature sugarcraft, fondant, piping, and creating 3D characters.

This show covers all sectors of

一場國際烘培展的記者會正在舉辦。

歡迎來到眾所期待，三年一度的烘培展。今年我們很驕傲地宣布參展廠商數量達到歷史新高，有來自 52 個國家共 665 家參展廠商。另外一個讓人興奮的消息是新的教育區，在教育區烘培大師將示範最新烘培技術，也將提供實際動手操作的研習課。以蛋糕裝飾技術為例，焦點有塑糖工藝、翻糖、花飾及 3D 角色製作。

這次展覽涵蓋了烘培產

222

備課、教學零煩惱 (教師適用)

★ 「分類話題」和「單句口譯」練習均適合老師於**口譯、口說、聽力**課上課中使用，請學生上講台播放CD後，請同學將聽到的內容翻成中文，再請另一同學翻回英文，達到中英雙向口譯練習。

★ 期中、期末考試抽考亦適用。

★ 請同學收集相關類別的展場，並做練習

❶ The sector covers baking tools and pastry ingredients.

❷ Professional pastry chefs will demonstrate intricate techniques.

❸ Sugarcraft and fondant have become the most popular cake decorating techniques.

❹ This bakery show offers the largest B2B trade platform in the related industry in Asia.

❺ The integrated bakery show encompasses a wide spectrum of sectors.

❻ The topics of the speeches range from marketing to logistics.

❼ It is quite an eye-opener to attend the seminar on the latest trend of baking.

❽ The show gathers bakery owners, food manufacturers, and bakery institutions.

224

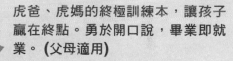

虎爸、虎媽的終極訓練本，讓孩子贏在終點。勇於開口說，畢業即就業。(父母適用)

★ 充分利用孩子黃金學習期，不花補習費，一次學習到位。

★ 抽考孩子各主題單字跟各單句英譯中等，有效檢視孩子學習成果。

大學生寒暑假不花錢的自修規劃首選書，訓練口譯自己來就行!!! (學生適用)

★ 與同學或朋友兩兩一組做「分類話題」和「單句口譯」練習，播放音檔後其中一人做英翻中練習，另一人則檢視對方翻譯內容，或將聽到的內容轉換成英文。

★ 每個單元內容都熟悉後，可以收集相關資料做延伸學習，更充分的打好口譯基礎。

目次

CONTENTS

① PART・設計類

設計展 01　紐約秋冬女鞋展 the New York Shoe Expo　016

設計展 02　畢業生時尚展 the Graduate Catwalk Show　022

設計展 03　新一代設計展 the Young Designers' Exhibition　028

設計展 04　倫敦設計節 the London Design Festival　034

設計展 05　智慧型手機周邊商品展 Smartphone Accessory Exhibition　040

設計展 06　東京國際珠寶展 International Jewelry Tokyo　046

設計展 07　深圳國際工業設計展 the Shenzhen International Industrial Design Fair　052

設計展 08 拉斯維加斯消費電子展 the Consumer Electronics Show in Las Vegas　058

設計展 09 巴黎家具家飾展 Maison & Object in Paris　064

② PART・建築類

建築展 10 莫斯科國際建材暨家飾展- part 1 Mosbuild International Exhibition of Building and Finishing Materials　072

建築展 11 莫斯科國際建材暨家飾展- part 2 Mosbuild International Exhibition of Building and Finishing Materials　078

目次 CONTENTS

建築展 12　上海國際智能家居展覽會 Shanghai Smart Home Technology　084

建築展 13　德國建築設計展 German Architecture and Design Exhibition　090

建築展 14　台灣國際建築及空間設計展 Taiwan International Architecture and Space Design Expo　096

建築展 15　建商商品介紹會 Builders' Merchandise Fair　102

建築展 16　華山文創園區綠建築展 Green Building Exhibition, Huashan Creative Park　108

建築展 17　上海永續建築展 Shanghai Sustainable Building Expo　114

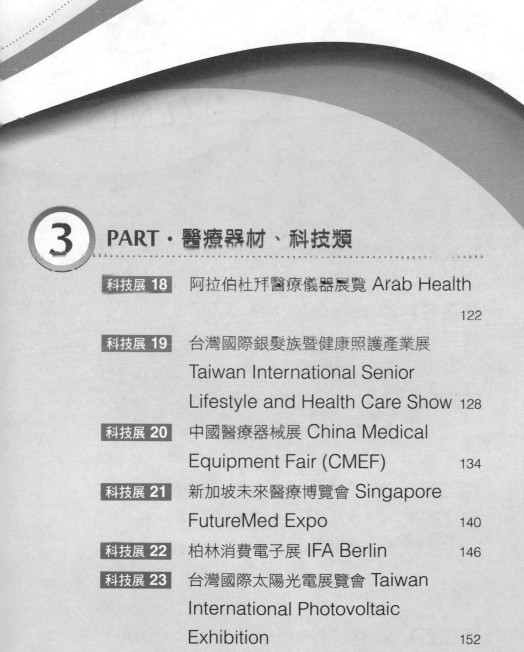

3 PART · 醫療器材、科技類

科技展 18　阿拉伯杜拜醫療儀器展覽 Arab Health

122

科技展 19　台灣國際銀髮族暨健康照護產業展
Taiwan International Senior
Lifestyle and Health Care Show　128

科技展 20　中國醫療器械展 China Medical
Equipment Fair (CMEF)　　134

科技展 21　新加坡未來醫療博覽會 Singapore
FutureMed Expo　　140

科技展 22　柏林消費電子展 IFA Berlin　　146

科技展 23　台灣國際太陽光電展覽會 Taiwan
International Photovoltaic
Exhibition　　152

目次

CONTENTS

科技展 **24** 美國地熱能協會地熱能博覽會 GEA GeoExpo 158

科技展 **25** 亞洲永續能源科技展 SETA (Sustainable Energy and Technology Asia) 164

科技展 **26** 台灣國際綠色產業展 Taiwan International Green Industry Show 170

科技展 **27** 東京車展 Tokyo Motor Show 176

科技展 **28** 國際食品加工及製藥機械展 International Food Processing & Pharmaceutical Machinery Show 182

科技展 **29** 亞太電子商務展 e-Commerce Expo Asia 188

科技展 **30** 半導體應用科普展 Semiconductor Application Exhibition　194

科技展 **31** 日本國際穿戴式裝置科技展 Wearable Device & Technology Expo　200

(4) PART・飯店、餐飲類

科技展 **32** 國際飯店展 International Hotel Show　208

科技展 **33** 飯店管理科系招生介紹 Hospitality Management Program　214

科技展 **34** 國際烘培展 International Bakery Show　220

科技展 **35** 台北國際茶與咖啡展 Taipei International Tea and Coffee Show　226

目次

CONTENTS

科技展 36 香港飯店管理培訓 Hotel Training Program in Hong Kong 　232

科技展 37 台北國際食品展 Taipei International Food Show 　238

⑤ PART · 國貿類

科技展 38 印尼雅加達家庭用品暨家飾展 Indonesia Housewares Fair Jakarta 　246

科技展 39 芝加哥家庭用品展 The International Home & Housewares Show Chicago 　252

科技展 40 英國國際禮品暨時尚生活用品展 Top Drawer London 　258

科技展 **41** 東京國際春季禮品展 Tokyo International Gift Show Spring　264

科技展 **42** 美國手工藝品展 The Craft & Hobby World Fair　270

科技展 **43** 香港玩具展 Hong Kong Toys & Games Fair　276

科技展 **44** 台北寵物用品展 Taipei Pets Show　282

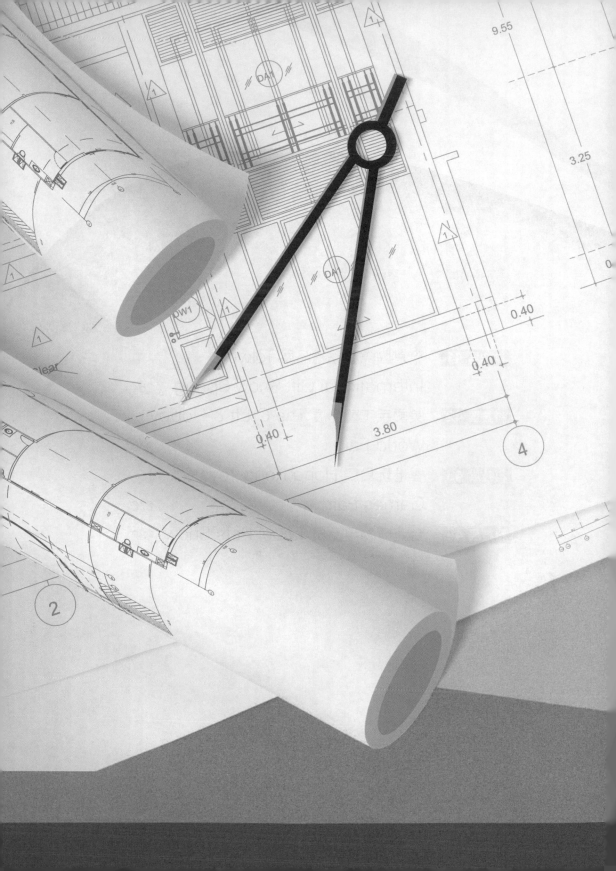

PART 1

設計類
篇章概述

設計展包含極廣，讀者可以先從精選的這九個展做練習，先
熟悉每個展別的常見字彙，再分別作單句和段落口譯練習。

01

設計展

紐約秋冬女鞋展
the New York Shoe Expo

口譯專業字彙 基礎字彙

字彙	音標	詞性	中譯
platforms	[`plæt͵fɔrmz]	n.	前台厚底鞋
trendsetter	[`trɛnd͵sɛtɚ]	n.	創造或引領潮流者
array	[ə`re]	n.	系列
sheepskin	[`ʃip͵skɪn]	n.	羊皮
texture	[`tɛkstʃɚ]	n.	質感
hand-sewn	[`hænd͵son]	adj.	手工縫紉的
embellish	[ɪm`bɛlɪʃ]	v.	裝飾
ankle	[`æŋk!]	n.	足踝
buckle	[`bʌk!]	n.	飾釦、搭鉤
loafers	[`lofɚz]	n.	樂福鞋
pumps	[pʌmps]	n.	淺口有跟女鞋
floral	[`florəl]	adj.	花卉圖案的
nonskid	[nɑn`skɪd]	adj.	防滑的
sole	[sol]	n.	鞋底
clogs	[klɑgz]	n.	圓頭無跟厚底鞋
ridge	[rɪdʒz]	n.	（防滑的）突起條紋

口譯專業字彙　進階字彙

字彙	音標	詞性	中譯
eponymous	[ɪ`pɑnəməs]	*adj.*	同名的
de rigueur	[də rɪ`gɝ]	*adj.*	時尚或禮節必需的
swatch	[swɑtʃ]	*n.*	樣品、樣本
sculptural	[`skʌlptʃərəl]	*adj.*	雕刻的
bejeweled	[bɪ`dʒuəld]	*adj.*	以珠寶裝飾的
avant-garde	[ɑvɑŋ`gɑrd]	*adj.*	前衛的
stiletto	[stɪ`lɛto]	*n.*	細高跟
wedge	[wɛdʒ]	*n.*	楔形跟
bespoke	[bɪ`spok]	*adj.*	訂製的
vamp	[væmp]	*n.*	鞋面
embroidered	[ɪm`brɔɪdəd]	*adj.*	刺繡的
embossed	[ɪm`bɑst]	*adj.*	壓印花紋的
overlay	[`ovɚ`le]	*n.*	裝飾片
mules	[mjulz]	*n.*	裸跟鞋
moccasins	[`mɑkəsnz]	*n.*	莫卡辛軟皮鞋
espadrilles	[`ɛspə͵drɪlz]	*n.*	草編鞋底涼鞋或帆布鞋

▶ New York Shoe Expo　紐約鞋類博覽會

The publicist for footwear designer, Mina Huang, is introducing the major fall and winter trends of the designer's eponymous brand in a press conference in the New York Shoe Expo held by FFANY (Fashion Footwear Association of New York).

鞋類設計師 Mina Huang 的公關人員正在紐約鞋類博覽會的記者會介紹設計師同名品牌的主要秋冬流行趨勢；紐約鞋類博覽會是由紐約時尚鞋類協會舉辦。

As a trendsetter in the women's footwear industry, Mina Huang brings you the trendiest footwear styles for fall and winter 2017. Luxury is the key, as you might have noticed from the array of posh and polished shoes on display. Consumers will easily find the right pairs for a variety of occasions, be it casual or formal.

身為女性鞋類產業的潮流創造者，Mina Huang 為您帶來 2017 年秋冬最潮的鞋類時尚。從展出的這一系列奢華雅致女鞋，您可能已經注意到，奢華是重點。消費者很容易就找到適合各種場合的鞋類，不管是休閒或正式場合。

For party goers, Mina Huang's

Mina Huang 的高跟

high-heel ankle boots, knee-high boots, or thigh-high boots will make you the center of the spotlight, as some of these boots are made with embossed leather, and the others are bejeweled or embellished with fur. On casual occasions, consumers can choose from clogs and moccasins covered by floral print overlays.

All of Mina Huang's shoes are made with supreme sheepskin and non-skid soles, so they not only dazzle people with their exquisite design, but also fit like a glove because of the soft texture.

踝靴、及膝靴或大腿靴能讓參加派對的人成為焦點，因為這些靴子有的以印花皮革製成，有的以珠寶或軟毛裝飾。在休閒場合，消費者可以選擇以花卉圖案裝飾片覆蓋的圓頭無跟厚底鞋及莫卡辛軟皮鞋。

所有 Mina Huang 的鞋子都是以最高級的羊皮及防滑鞋根製作，所以它們不只精緻的設計讓人讚嘆不已，也因柔軟的質感，穿著感覺非常舒適。

設計類

1

建築類

2

醫療器材、科技類

3

飯店、餐飲類

4

國貿類

5

1 As a trendsetter in avant-garde fashion, footwear designer Eric Wu released his latest series of high-heel boots.

2 The series was inspired by 3D printing technology.

3 The heels are embellished with sculptural details made with 3D printing technology.

4 The exquisite heels are sure to catch everyone's eye.

5 Some of these heels are stilettos, while the others are wedges.

6 These boots are de rigueur / fashion must-haves this season.

7 The series combines art and technology.

8 Consumers wearing these boots will feel up-to-date on the hottest fashion.

設計類

1

建築類

2

科技類　醫療器材、

3

餐飲類　飯店、

4

國貿類

5

❶ 身為前衛潮流的引領著，鞋類設計師 Eric Wu 推出他的最新高跟皮靴系列。

❷ 這系列受到 3D 列印科技啟發。

❸ 鞋跟以 3D 列印科技製作的雕刻細節裝飾。

❹ 精緻的鞋跟一定會吸引每個人的注意。

❺ 有些鞋跟是細高跟，有些是楔形跟。

❻ 這些皮靴是這一季時尚必備的 / 時尚必需品。

❼ 這系列結合藝術與科技。

❽ 穿著這些皮靴的消費者會覺得走在潮流的尖端。

設計展

畢業生時尚展 the Graduate Catwalk Show

口譯專業字彙　基礎字彙

字彙	音標	詞性	中譯
gown	[gaʊn]	n.	女性晚禮服
inspire	[ɪnˋspaɪr]	v.	激發靈感
strive	[straɪv]	v.	努力
synthetic	[sɪnˋθɛtɪk]	adj.	合成的
fiber	[ˋfaɪbɚ]	n.	纖維
opt for	[ɑpt fɔr]	v. phr.	選擇
organic	[ɔrˋgænɪk]	adj.	有機的
dye	[daɪ]	v., n.	染色、染料
indigo	[ˋɪnˌdɪgo]	n., adj.	靛藍
annatto	[əˋnɑto]	n.	胭脂樹紅
motif	[moˋtif]	n.	主題
strut	[strʌt]	v.	昂首闊步
flutter	[ˋflʌtɚ]	v.	飄動
delicate	[ˋdɛləkɪt]	adj.	精美的
reflect	[rɪˋflɛkt]	v.	反映
craftsmanship	[ˋkræftsmənˌʃɪp]	n.	技藝

口譯專業字彙　進階字彙

字彙	音標	詞性	中譯
haute couture	[ot ku`tʊr]	*n.*	高級訂製時裝
outfit	[`aʊt͵fɪt]	*n.*	全套服裝
apparel	[ə`pærəl]	*n.*	衣服
denim	[`dɛnɪm]	*n.*	丹寧布
anorak	[`anə͵rak]	*n.*	連帽厚夾克
cardigan	[`kardɪgən]	*n.*	開襟羊毛衫
nylon	[`naɪlɑn]	*n.*	尼龍
polyester	[͵pɑlɪ`ɛstɚ]	*n.*	聚酯纖維
checked	[tʃɛkt]	*adj.*	格子化紋的
polka dot	[`polkə dɑt]	*n.*	圓點花樣
stripe	[straɪp]	*n.*	條紋
tartan	[`tɑrtn]	*n.*	格子呢
vintage	[`vɪntɪdʒ]	*n.*	復古風、古著、古董
silhouette	[͵sɪlʊ`ɛt]	*n.*	輪廓
drip-dry	[drɪp draɪ]	*adj.*	快乾的
asymmetric	[͵æsɪ`mɛtrɪk]	*adj.*	不對稱的

設計類
1
建築類
2
醫療器材、科技類
3
飯店、餐飲類
4
國貿類
5

A student in the Department of Fashion Design of Best University is introducing her collection in the Graduate Catwalk Show.

一名倍斯特大學流行服飾設計系的學生正在畢業生時尚展介紹她的服裝系列。

The idea behind the collection of evening gowns was inspired by the global trend of rethinking humans' relationship with nature, and; therefore, we strove to keep the manufacturing process as natural as possible.

這一系列晚禮服的靈感是來自於重新思考人類和自然的關係這股全球趨勢，因此我們努力將製造過程維持極盡天然。

We reduced the amount of synthetic fiber and opted for organic cotton and silk. Vegetable dyes were applied to the background colors. Even the dye materials were collected from local plants; for example, as you can see, the background color brown was produced from lychee leaves, the blue from

我們減少了合成纖維的數量及選擇有機棉和蠶絲。植物性染料被應用在衣服的底色。甚至染料都是取材自本土植物。例如，這裡你看到的，咖啡色底色是由荔枝葉製作，藍色來自木蘭，而金橘色來自胭脂樹種子。

indigo plants, and the golden orange from annatto seeds.

Each gown carries a plant motif, so it seems that the gown grows out of nature itself. Take the major patterns on these three gowns for instance, this one carries bamboo leaves and branches on the skirt. As the model struts down the catwalk, it looks as if the leaves flutter in the wind. The other two gowns carry azaleas and peonies. These delicate patterns are embroidered by hand, reflecting superb craftsmanship.

每件晚禮服都有植物的主題，所以看來好像是發源自大自然。例如這三件的主要圖案，這件裙子上有竹葉和樹枝圖案。當模特兒在伸展台闊步時，看來好像樹葉在風中搖擺。另外這兩件晚禮服有杜鵑及牡丹的主題。這些細緻的圖案是由手工刺繡而成，也反映出高級的技藝。

❶ The asymmetric neckline grabs people's attention.

❷ Haute couture from Dior is highly anticipated.

❸ Checked trench coats are the mainstream in the fall-winter fashion this year.

❹ Denim never goes out of style.

❺ Vintage apparel dominate the catwalk this season.

❻ Cardigans and blouses of various colors always match well.

❼ With some accessories, this dress will look more like a complete outfit.

❽ More and more casual clothing brands are adopting organic cotton.

❶ 這個不對稱的領口能吸引眾人的目光。

❷ Dior 的高級訂製時裝令人高度期待。

❸ 格子花紋的風衣是今年秋冬流行的主流。

❹ 單寧布料永遠不會退流行。

❺ 復古風的衣服佔領了這一季的伸展台。

❻ 不同顏色的開襟羊毛衫和女士襯衫總是能搭配地不錯。

❼ 搭配一些配件，這件洋裝看來比較像一套完整的服裝。

❽ 越來越多休閒服飾品牌採用有機棉。

03

新一代設計展 the Young Designers' Exhibition

口譯專業字彙　基礎字彙

字彙	音標	詞性	中譯
affordable	[əˋfɔrdəb!]	adj.	負擔得起的
budget-conscious	[ˋbʌdʒɪt ˋkɑnʃəs]	adj.	注意預算的
lampshade	[ˋlæmp,ʃed]	n.	燈罩
formative	[ˋfɔrmətɪv]	adj.	構成的
property	[ˋprɑpə-tɪ]	n.	特性
versatile	[ˋvɝsət!]	adj.	多功能的、易變的
bulb	[bʌlb]	n.	燈泡
interior	[ɪnˋtɪrɪə-]	adj. n.	內部
unfold	[ʌnˋfold]	v.	攤開、展開
manual	[ˋmænjʊəl]	n.	手冊
assemble	[əˋsɛmb!]	v.	組裝
disassemble	[,dɪsəˋsɛmb!]	v.	拆卸
lighting	[ˋlaɪtɪŋ]	n.	照明設備
illumination	[ɪ,ljuməˋneʃən]	n.	彩燈、燈飾
beam	[bim]	n.	光束
dimmer	[ˋdɪmə-]	n.	調光器

口譯專業字彙　進階字彙

字彙	音標	詞性	中譯
incandescent	[ˌɪnkænˋdɛsnt]	adj.	白熱的
chandelier	[ˌʃændlˋɪr]	n.	枝形吊燈
fixture	[ˋfɪkstʃɚ]	n.	固定裝置
fluorescent	[fluəˋrɛsnt]	adj.	螢光的
lumen	[ˋlumən]	n.	流明
luminous	[ˋlumənəs]	adj.	照亮的
floodlight	[ˋflʌdˌlaɪt]	n.	泛光燈
strip light	[strɪp laɪt]	n.	條狀照明燈
illuminance	[ɪˋlumənəns]	n.	照明度
pendant	[ˋpɛndənt]	n.	吊燈
sconce	[skɑns]	n.	壁燈
canopy	[ˋkænəpɪ]	n.	篷形遮蓋物
cylinder	[ˋsɪlɪndɚ]	n.	圓柱
stained glass	[stend glæs]	n.	彩繪玻璃
tiered	[tɪrd]	adj.	疊層的
crystal	[ˋkrɪstl]	n., adj.	水晶

設計類

1

建築類

2

醫療器材、科技類

3

飯店、餐飲類

4

國貿類

5

A student participating in YODEX (the Young Designers' Exhibition) is explaining the concept of his lamp design.

一位參加新一代設計展的學生正在解釋他的桌燈設計概念。

As many of you know, living in a big city involves high rent and small space. So, the concept of my design arose from an attempt to develop lamps that not only are affordable to those who are budget-conscious, but also occupy just a little storage space.

如同你們許多人知道的，住在大都市牽涉到高房租和小空間。所以我的設計概念源自於嘗試針對在意預算的人，發展不只是負擔得起，也只佔一點點收納空間的燈具。

Our team used PET sheets as the base material for the lampshade. The formative and lightweight properties of PET sheets allowed us to develop versatile shapes of lampshades.

我們的團隊使用 PET 聚酯片材當作燈罩的基底。PET 聚酯片材的易塑性及輕量的特質使我們能研發各種形狀的燈罩。

As you can see, the whole set of

如同您看到的，整組燈

lamp comes in a small box, which includes a bulb base, two LED light bulbs, and three PET sheets that can be folded into lampshades of different shapes and colors. Consumers can change the lampshade easily to match individual interior design.

When unfolded, the sheets are as thin as a piece of paper, and thus can be stored anywhere. Of course, the set also includes a manual to guide users through how to assemble and disassemble the lamp. The steps are fairly simple—you can assemble it even without reading the manual.

具可收到一個小盒子，包括一個燈泡底座，兩個 LED 燈泡，和三個不同顏色的 PET 片材，能折成不同形狀的燈罩。消費者能輕易地更換燈罩，以搭配個別的室內設計。

攤開來的時候，這些 PET 片材的厚度和紙一樣薄，因此能隨處收納。當然，整組也包括一份說明書，引導使用者如何組裝和拆卸桌燈。步驟其實很簡單─甚至不讀說明書，你也會組裝。

設計類

建築類

1

2

醫療器材、科技類

3

飯店、餐飲類

4

國貿類

5

❶ The lampshade looks like a big canopy, and the light illuminates the whole room once switched on.

❷ This metal pendant creates an intensive visual effect.

❸ These spherical sconces look like installation art works, instilling joy into an ordinary space.

❹ Numerous dots on this hollow out steel lampshade were cut by laser, and they form the flowery pattern.

❺ Crystal chandeliers are indispensable in banquet halls.

❻ Cloud shaped pendants bring elements of nature into the interior space.

❼ The series of ceramic and porcelain lighting was inspired by coffee cups, and they come in white, orange, and beige.

❽ Consumers can mix and match hand blown glass pendants of various colors by themselves.

1 燈罩外型宛如一頂大帳篷，一打開燈馬上照亮整個房間。

2 這座金屬吊燈在視覺上造成強烈的效果。

3 這幾盞球形壁燈看來就像是裝置藝術品，將平凡的空間注入樂趣。

4 這個鏤空鋼質燈罩的眾多小點由雷射切割，這些點組合成花的圖案。

5 水晶枝形吊燈在晚宴廳是不可或缺的。

6 雲朵造型吊燈將大自然元素帶入室內空間。

7 這一陶瓷燈具系列靈感來自於咖啡杯，顏色有白色，橙色和米色。

8 消費者可以自行混搭不同顏色的手工吹製玻璃吊燈。

04

設計展

倫敦設計節 the London Design Festival

口譯專業字彙　基礎字彙

字彙	音標	詞性	中譯
tableware	[ˋtebl͵wɛr]	n.	餐具（總稱）
silicone	[ˋsɪlɪ͵kon]	n.	矽膠、矽樹脂
collapsible	[kəˋlæpsəbl]	adj.	可摺疊的
leakproof	[ˋlik͵pruf]	adj.	防漏的
infuser	[ɪnˋfjuzɚ]	n.	泡茶器
brew	[bru]	v.	釀造、泡茶
emerald	[ˋɛmərəld]	n., adj.	祖母綠
crimson	[ˋkrɪmzn]	n., adj.	深紅色
maize	[mez]	n., adj.	玉米色
turquoise	[ˋtɝkwɔɪz]	n., adj.	藍綠色、土耳其綠
ceramic	[səˋræmɪk]	adj.	陶器的
porcelain	[ˋpɔrslɪn]	n.	瓷
resistant	[rɪˋzɪstənt]	adj.	抗拒的
integrated	[ˋɪntə͵gretɪd]	adj.	整合的、一體成形的
peg	[pɛg]	n.	椿型掛勾
spillover	[ˋspɪl͵ovɚ]	n.	溢出

口譯專業字彙　進階字彙

字彙	音標	詞性	中譯
curve	[kɝv]	n.	弧線、弧度
minimalist	[`mɪnəməlɪst]	adj.	極簡風格的
pepper mill	[`pɛpɚ mɪl]	n.	磨胡椒子的小罐
salt shaker	[sɔlt ʃekɚ]	n..	灑鹽罐
crockery	[`krɑkərɪ]	n.	陶器（總稱）
flatware	[`flæt ˌwɛr]	n.	扁平的餐具（總稱）
goblet	[`gɑblɪt]	n.	高腳杯
cutlery	[`kʌtlərɪ]	n.	餐具（總稱）
culinary	[`kjulɪ ˌnɛrɪ]	adj.	烹飪的
biodegradable	[`baɪodɪ`gredəbl]	adj.	可生物分解的
utensil	[ju`tɛnsl]	n.	器皿
lacquer	[`lækɚ]	n.	漆器
anti-topple	[`æntɪ tɑpl]	adj.	防傾倒的
tumbler	[`tʌmblɚ]	n.	平底無腳酒杯
gadgetry	[`gædʒətrɪ]	n.	小玩意、小機件
silverware	[`sɪlvɚ ˌwɛr]	n.	銀器

A tableware designer from Taiwan is giving a short presentation on his set of tableware in the London Design Festival.

來自台灣的餐具設計師正在倫敦設計節簡短陳述介紹他的一組餐具。

The set of silicone tableware is designed to be fun, highly-functional, and safe. The set includes 1 collapsible kettle, 4 collapsible cups, 4 leakproof lids, and 4 tea infusers.

這組矽膠餐具的設計用意是有趣，高功能及安全。整組包含一個可摺疊的茶壺，四個可摺疊杯子，四個防漏杯蓋及四個泡茶器。

They bring a creative aspect to the traditional art of tea brewing, and come in a variety of bright colors, such as emerald green, crimson red, maize yellow and turquoise blue. So, consumers can enjoy the fun of mixing and matching various colors.

它們替傳統茶藝帶來創意，而且有多樣色彩，例如翠玉綠、深紅色、玉米黃及藍綠色。所以消費者能享受混搭顏色的樂趣。

Unlike traditional kettles that are

不像傳統茶壺以陶瓷製

made of ceramic and porcelain, our tableware utilizes highly heat-resistant, BPA free, and food-grade silicone rubber. Under the lids, you can see the small integrated pegs to which you can hang the infusers.

When you are on the go, just cover the cup with the leakproof lid and don't need to worry a bit about spillover. The portable nature of silicone makes them fit in a backpack or handbag, since when collapsed, the kettle and cups are only 5 centimeters and 2 centimeters high, and when unfolded, 20 centimeters and 8 centimeters, respectively holding 1.5 liters and 350 ml.

作，我們的餐具使用高耐熱，不含雙酚 A 的食品級矽膠。在杯蓋下，有一體成型的小掛勾，可以將泡茶器掛著。

當你在行動中，只要蓋上防漏杯蓋就不用擔心漏出。矽膠易攜帶的特質使整組餐具能收到背包或手提袋裡，因為摺疊時，茶壺和杯子只有五公分及兩公分高，展開時，則是二十公分及八公分高，容量則分別是 1.5 公升及 350 毫升。

設計類

1

建築類

2

醫療器材、科技類

3

飯店、餐飲類

4

國貿類

5

❶ The curves of these bowls and plates are specifically designed so that they can be stacked.

❷ The bottoms of these plates and trays are coated with nonskid finish.

❸ The set of minimalist cutlery for children was made of food-grade silicone rubber.

❹ This food-grade silicone kettle comes with a stainless steel base.

❺ Anti-topple cups can enhance the safety when they are used by the elder and children.

❻ The slightly bent portion at the end of the spoons caters to right and left-handed grasping positions.

❼ This set of portable stainless steel cutlery includes a pair of chopsticks, a spoon, and a fork, all of which are collapsible.

❽ Using black lacquer utensils to hold food seems particularly poetic.

設計類

1

建築類

2

科技類 醫療器材、

3

餐飲類 飯店、

4

國貿類

5

❶ 這些碗和盤子的弧度經過特殊設計,可以堆疊在一起。

❷ 這些盤子和托盤底部都有止滑表面處理。

❸ 這組極簡風的兒童餐具使用食品級矽膠製作。

❹ 這個食品級的矽膠菜壺附有不銹鋼底座。

❺ 防傾倒的杯子能增加老年人及兒童使用時的安全。

❻ 這些湯匙尾端稍微彎曲的部分迎合了右撇子和左撇子的手持姿勢。

❼ 這組不銹鋼攜帶型餐具組包括一雙筷子,一支湯匙和一支叉子,全部都可以摺疊。

❽ 使用黑色漆器的器皿承裝食物看來特別有詩意。

05

智慧型手機周邊商品展 Smartphone Accessory Exhibition

口譯專業字彙　基礎字彙

字彙	音標	詞性	中譯
lithium	[ˋlɪθɪəm]	n.	鋰
dual	[ˋdjuəl]	adj.	雙重的
anti-scratch	[ˋæntɪ skrætʃ]	adj.	防刮的
shockproof	[ˋʃɑk͵pruf]	adj.	防震的
durable	[ˋdjʊrəb!]	adj.	耐用的
frame	[frem]	n.	邊框
grip	[grɪp]	v., n.	緊握
camouflage	[ˋkæmə͵flɑʒ]	n., v.	偽裝、迷彩色
matte	[mæt]	adj., n.	霧面的
plug adapter	[plʌg əˋdæptɚ]	n.	轉接頭
accessory	[ækˋsɛsərɪ]	n.	配件、周邊商品
selfie	[sɛlfɪ]	n.	自拍照
integrate	[ˋɪntə͵gret]	v.	結合
portable	[ˋportəb!]	adj.	可攜的
embody	[ɪmˋbɑdɪ]	v.	包含
compatible	[kəmˋpætəb!]	adj.	相容的

口譯專業字彙　進階字彙

字彙	音標	詞性	中譯
polymer	[`pɑlɪmɚ]	*n.*	聚合物
armband	[`ɑrm͵bænd]	*n.*	臂套
touchscreen	[`tʌtʃ͵skrin]	*n.*	觸控螢幕
stylus	[`staɪləs]	*n.*	觸控筆
configure	[kən`fɪgɚ]	*v.*	配置
multicast	[`mʌltɪ͵kast]	*n.*	多重播送
compatibility	[kəm͵pætə`bɪlətɪ]	*n*	相容性
protective film	[prə`tɛktɪv fɪlm]	*adj.+n*	保護膜
tempered glass	[`tɛmpɚd glæs]	*adj.+n.*	強化玻璃
screen protector	[skrin prə`tɛktɚ]	*n.*	螢幕保護貼
resistive	[rɪ`zɪstɪv]	*adj.*	電阻式
capacitive	[kə`pæsətɪv]	*adj.*	電容式
tethering	[`tɛðɚɪŋ]]	*n.*	網路共享
mobile hotspot	[`mobɪl `hɑtspɑt]	*adj.+n.*	移動熱點
standalone	[`stændə͵lon]	*adj.*	獨立式的
headset	[`hɛd͵sɛt]	*n.*	頭戴裝置

設計類
建築類
科技類 醫療器材、
餐飲類 飯店、
國貿類
1 2 3 4 5

A student who majors in Industrial Design is giving a presentation on his dual function cell phone case.

一位主修工業設計系的學生正在介紹他設計的雙重功能手機套。

Hello, everyone, I'm proud to present to you the dual function cell phone case. First, I'd like to fill you in on what inspired my design. I noticed lots of people like to go jogging and listen to music at the same time, and it's quite a bummer if the music stops because the battery dies.

大家好，我很榮幸能向你們呈現這個雙重功能手機套。首先，我想提一下是什麼啟發了我的設計。我注意到很多人喜歡一邊慢跑，一邊聽音樂。如果因為電池沒電，音樂停了，那是很掃興的事。

Or you might have had the experience in which your phone conversation unfortunately got cut off because your battery was dead. Well, with this dual function phone case, you can rest assured that the awkward situation won't happen again.

或者你可能有這種經驗，你在手機上聊天，但不幸地因電池沒電而被迫中斷談話。嗯，有了這個雙重功能手機套，你可以放心這個尷尬的狀況不會再發生。

42

The case integrates a Bluetooth speaker and a portable charger with a built-in 5000mAh lithium polymer battery. Because of the streamlined design, most people wouldn't notice it embodies extra functions. Feel free to hold it—you'll find it's really light. The case is made of durable rubber with matte finish, which is anti-scratch and shockproof, and the TPU bumper frame offers firm grip. It is available in three colors, black, red, and camouflage, and is compatible with iPhone 7 only.

這手機套整合了一個藍芽喇叭和內建 5000mAh 鋰聚合電池的行動電源。因為流線型的設計，大部份的人不會注意到它有額外功能。歡迎拿拿看一你會發現他真的很輕。這個手機套是以耐久的橡膠製作，表面有霧面處理，也有防刮及防震處理，TPU 防撞邊框提供穩定的手持手感。有三個顏色可選擇，黑色、紅色及迷彩色，只跟 iPhone 7 相容。

設計類 1
建築類 2
醫療器材、科技類 3
飯店、餐飲類 4
國貿類 5

❶ With this versatile cell phone case, you don't even need to bring a portable charger when you go out.

❷ This cell phone case and wallet are integrated.

❸ This 2-in-1 cell phone case can accommodate credit cards and cash.

❹ The high quality faux leather cell phone case with soft touch is a fashion accessory.

❺ Cell phone armbands must provide an excellent shockproof function.

❻ Look at the delicate stitching on the edges of the leather case.

❼ Foldable selfie sticks are portable and convenient during travelling.

❽ The tempered glass screen protector protects your precious cell phone.

1 有了這個多功能手機套，出門時連行動電源都不用帶。

2 這個手機套和皮夾結合。

3 這個二合一的手機套可收納信用卡和現金。

4 觸感柔軟的高級仿皮手機套是個時尚配件。

5 手機臂套必須提供優良的防震功能。

6 看看這皮套邊緣精美的縫線。

7 可折疊的自拍棒方便旅遊時攜帶。

8 強化玻璃的螢幕保護貼保護您珍貴的手機。

設計類 **1**

建築類 **2**

科技類、醫療器材 **3**

飯店、餐飲類 **4**

國貿類 **5**

06

設計展

東京國際珠寶展
International Jewelry Tokyo

口譯專業字彙　基礎字彙

字彙	音標	詞性	中譯
pendant	[ˋpɛndənt]	n.	垂飾
carve	[kɑrv]	v.	雕刻
sterling silver	[ˋstɚ·lɪŋ ˋsɪlvɚ]	n.	紋銀、925 銀
geometric	[dʒɪəˋmɛtrɪk]	adj.	幾何的
glitz	[glɪts]	n.	耀眼
glamour	[ˋglæmɚ]	n.	魅力
accentuate	[ækˋsɛntʃuˏet]	v.	強調
zircon	[ˋzɚ·kɑn]	n.	鋯石
embed	[ɪmˋbɛd]	v.	鑲嵌
gemstone	[ˋdʒɛmˏston]	n.	寶石
aura	[ˋɔrə]	n.	氣息
posture	[ˋpɑstʃɚ]	n.	姿態
refraction	[rɪˋfrækʃn]	n.	折射
symbol	[ˋsɪmb!]	n.	象徵
attire	[əˋtaɪr]	n.	服裝
brooch	[brotʃ]	n.	胸針

口譯專業字彙　進階字彙

字彙	音標	詞性	中譯
facet	[`fæsɪt]	n.	鑽石的小平面
sapphire	[`sæfaɪr]	n.	藍寶石
inlay	[`ɪn‚le]	n.	鑲嵌物、鑲嵌圖案
bangle	[`bæŋg!]	n.	手鐲、腳鐲
locket	[`lɑkɪt]	n.	小盒子形狀的鏈墜
medallion	[mɪ`dæljən]	n.	圓形雕飾
topaz	[`topæz]	n	黃晶
opal	[`op!]	n.	蛋白石
translucent	[træns`lusnt]	adj.	半透明的
aquamarine	[‚ækwəmə`rin]	n.	藍晶
amethyst	[`æməθɪst]	n.	紫水晶
agate	[`ægət]	n.	瑪瑙
onyx	[`ɑnɪks]	n.	縞瑪瑙
garnet	[`gɑrnɪt]	n.	石榴石
cameo	[`kæmɪ‚o]	n.	多彩浮雕寶石
burnish	[`bɝnɪʃ]	v., n.	磨光、光澤

A jewelry designer from Taiwan is introducing her latest series in IJT (International Jewelry Tokyo).

All of the pendants and rings in the minimalist animal series are hand carved and made of the finest sterling silver. The minimalist and geometric style does not reduce the glitz and glamour, but rather accentuates the zircons embedded as these animals' eyes.

The colors of zircons vary from one animal to another. Let me take the fox and the owl rings for example. Their eyes are emerald and sapphire blue zircon inlays respectively. Since every piece is hand carved, each exhibits a unique facial expression or posture. For instance, the long

一位來自台灣的珠寶設計師正在東京國際珠寶展介紹她的最新系列。

所有這一極簡風動物系列的垂飾及戒指都是由手工雕刻，以最高品質的 925 銀製作。極簡風和幾何風格並不會減少耀眼的光采及魅力，反而強調了鑲嵌為動物眼睛的鋯石。

每個動物造型搭配的鋯石顏色都不同。以狐狸和貓頭鷹戒指來說，它們的眼睛分別由祖母綠和藍寶鋯石鑲嵌。因為每件珠寶都是手工雕刻，每件都展現獨特的表情及姿態。例如，狐狸的脖子延伸至指環，

neck of the fox extends into the band, and wraps around the wearer's finger gently as if it's part of the finger.

The glittery refraction of the sapphire zircon adds an aura of sophistication to the owl, since owls are the symbol of wisdom.

Our rings and pendants complement both daily and formal attire. Each piece can be custom made, including the colors and types of gemstones. Or we can adjust the rings into earrings, pendants into brooches for you.

溫柔地圍繞手指好像它是手指的一部分。

因為貓頭鷹是智慧的象徵，藍寶鋯石耀眼的折射增加了貓頭鷹優雅的氣息。

我們的戒指及垂飾能搭配平日和正式服裝。每件可訂做，包括寶石的顏色和種類。或者我們能為您將戒指調整成耳環，垂飾調整成胸針。

設計類

1

建築類

2

醫療器材、科技類

3

飯店、餐飲類

4

國貿類

5

❶ Platinum rings are suitable for all occasions.

❷ The band of this ring is made from platinum because platinum is more durable than gold.

❸ The pearl necklace is the most iconic accessory to go with an evening gown.

❹ 1.5 carat pear shaped rings are gaining more popularity.

❺ These hand carved medallions can be adjusted into necklace pendants.

❻ The topaz inlays make this set of earrings glitzier.

❼ This bangle is hand made from sterling silver, and filled with delicate details.

❽ The sculpted multi-facets of this diamond enhance its dazzling refraction.

設計類
1
建築類
2
醫療器材、
科技類
3
飯店、
餐飲類
4
國貿類
5

❶ 柏金戒指適合各種場合穿戴。

❷ 這枚戒指的指環使用柏金打造，因為鉑金比黃金更耐用。

❸ 珍珠項鍊是搭配晚禮服最經典的配件。

❹ 1.5 克拉的梨形戒指越來越流行。

❺ 這些手工雕刻的圓形雕飾能被調整成項鍊的垂飾。

❻ 黃晶鑲嵌讓這組耳環更耀眼。

❼ 這只手環由 925 銀手工製作，充滿精緻的細節。

❽ 這顆鑽石的多面向切割加強了它耀眼的折射。

07

設計展

深圳國際工業設計展
the Shenzhen International Industrial Design Fair

口譯專業字彙　基礎字彙

字彙	音標	詞性	中譯
drone	[dron]	n.	無人機
scout	[skaʊt]	v., n.	偵查
niche	[nɪtʃ]	n.	壁龕、利基
unmanned	[ˌʌnˋmænd]	adj.	無人駕駛的
hover	[ˋhʌvɚ]	v.	盤旋
prototype	[ˋprotəˌtaɪp]	n.	原型
representative	[rɛprɪˋzɛntətɪv]	adj.	代表性的
utilize	[ˋjutḷˌaɪz]	v.	使用
altitude	[ˋæltəˌtjud]	n.	海拔高度
avoidance	[əˋvɔɪdəns]	n.	迴避
paramedic	[ˌpærəˋmɛdɪk]	n.	急救護理人員
compartment	[kəmˋpɑrtmənt]	n.	隔間
gridlock	[ˋgrɪdˌlɑk]	n.	交通堵塞
obstacle	[ˋɑbstəkḷ]	n.	障礙
mechanical	[məˋkænɪkḷ]	adj.	機械的
ambulance	[ˋæmbjələns]	n.	救護車

口譯專業字彙　進階字彙

字彙	音標	詞性	中譯
aviation	[ˌevɪˈeʃən]	*n.*	航空
propeller	[prəˈpɛlɚ]	*n.*	螺旋槳、推進器
rotor	[ˈrotɚ]	*n.*	旋轉輪、旋轉翼
vertical	[ˈvɝtɪkl̩]	*adj.*	垂直的
horizontal	[ˌhɑrəˈzɑntl̩]	*adj.*	水平的
aerial	[ˈɛrɪəl]	*adj.*	航空的
turbofan	[ˈtɝboˌfæn]	*n.*	渦輪風扇
traction	[ˈtrækʃən]	*n.*	牽引力
trajectory	[trəˈdʒɛktrɪ]	*n.*	軌跡
navigation	[ˌnævəˈgeʃən]	*n.*	航行
autonomous	[ɔˈtɑnəməs]	*adj.*	自動化的
alloy	[əˈlɔɪ]	*n.*	合金
orient	[ˈorɪˌɛnt]	*v.*	定位
levitate	[ˈlɛvəˌtet]	*v.*	升空、飄浮
gravity	[ˈgrævətɪ]	*n.*	重力
configuration	[kənˌfɪgjəˈreʃən]	*n.*	配置

設計類
1

建築類
2

醫療器材、科技類
3

飯店、餐飲類
4

國貿類
5

A brief introduction on an ambulance drone is being given in the Shenzhen International Industrial Design Fair.

關於無人駕駛救護機的簡短介紹正在深圳國際工業設計展進行中。

Ladies and gentlemen, the concept drone we present to you today is the world's first ever ambulance drone that carries immense potential to help solve current problems in the medical and transportation areas. While drones used in the delivery and military scouts are commonplace, they might still be perceived as belonging to niche hobbyists.

先生女士們，我們今天呈現的無人駕駛概念機是世界上第一台無人駕駛救護機，它蘊含極大潛力，能協助解決當今醫療和運輸的問題。雖然用於宅配和軍事偵查的無人機已經普遍，無人機可能仍被認為只屬於小眾玩家。

But we believe the future of drones applied in diversified industries will soon be a reality. Our prototype is representative of how drones can be utilized to speed up rescue. It is designed

但是我們相信無人機被應用於各項產業在未來很快就會成真。我們的原型可代表無人機如何加速急救。它被設計為低海拔高度飛行，並配

to fly in low altitude and equipped with obstacle avoidance technology.

It can carry at least the weight of two average adults-- assumingly, one paramedic and one patient -- as well as one stretcher. There is also a large compartment to hold rescue equipment.

Every second counts in rescue missions; guided by GPS to a cell phone location, drone ambulances will drastically increase patients' survival rate by avoiding surface gridlock.

備防障礙科技。

它能負載至少兩位平均成人的重量—預設的是一位救護員和一位病人—及一個擔架。也有一個大隔間能放置急救設備。

在急救任務中，每一秒都重要。無人駕駛救護機由 GPS 定位引導至手機位址，藉由避免地面交通堵塞，無人駕駛救護機將大幅地增加病人的存活率。

設計類

1

建築類

2

醫療器材、科技類

3

飯店、餐飲類

4

國貿類

5

❶ Unmanned aerial vehicles, also known as drones, will carry more creative usages in the future.

❷ Photographers often use drones to obtain unique aerial angles.

❸ Drones have often been applied to humanitarian rescue missions in the recent years.

❹ This enterprise pioneered in utilizing drones to deliver cargos.

❺ Drones can fly into storms, and collect meteorological data.

❻ The single passenger drone made its debut in this exhibition.

❼ The electric-powered drone can be fully charged in one hour.

❽ A low altitude air traffic control system will need to be built to avoid drone crashes.

① 無人駕駛的飛行器，又稱為無人機，在未來將有更多充滿創意的用途。

② 攝影師常常使用無人機以取得獨特的空拍角度。

③ 無人機近年來常被應用於人道緊急救援任務。

④ 這間企業率先使用無人機運送貨物。

⑤ 無人機能飛進暴風雨並收集氣象資料。

⑥ 可承載單人的自動駕駛飛行器首次在這次展覽亮相。

⑦ 這台充電型的無人機在一小時就能充滿電。

⑧ 低海拔高度的空中交通控制系統未來需要被建立，以避免無人機碰撞。

08

設計展

拉斯維加斯消費電子展 the Consumer Electronics Show in Las Vegas

口譯專業字彙　基礎字彙

字彙	音標	詞性	中譯
unveil	[ʌn`vel]	v.	揭露、揭幕
intelligent	[ɪn`tɛlədʒənt]	adj.	智能的
familiarize	[fə`mɪljə‚raɪz]	v.	使熟悉
amicable	[`æmɪkəb!]	adj.	友善的
voice-controlled	[vɔɪs kən`trold]	adj.	聲控的
individualize	[‚ɪndə`vɪdʒʊəl‚aɪz]	v.	個人化
calibrate	[`kælə‚bret]	v.	校正
rectangular	[rɛk`tæŋgjələ‑]	adj.	矩形的
equip	[ɪ`kwɪp]	v.	配備
robotic	[ro`bɑtɪk]	adj.	機器人的
surveillance	[sə‑`veləns]	n.	監看
connectivity	[kə‚nɛktɪvə‚tɪ]	n.	（網路）連線
built-in	[`bɪlt`ɪn]	adj.	內建的
device	[dɪ`vaɪs]	n.	裝置
sensor	[`sɛnsə‑]	n.	感應器
collision	[kə`lɪʒən]	n.	相撞

口譯專業字彙　　進階字彙

字彙	音標	詞性	中譯
humanoid	[`hjumənɔɪd]	n.	人形機器人
cyborg	[`saɪbɔrg]	n.	半人半機械的機械人
robotics	[roˋbɑtɪks]	n.	機器人學
articulation	[ɑrˌtɪkjəˋleʃən]	n.	以類關節連接的裝置
axis	[`æksɪs]	n.	軸
welding	[wɛldɪŋ]	n.	焊接
rotation	[roˋteʃən]	n.	旋轉
elevation	[ˌɛləˋveʃən]	n	升高
acceleration	[ækˌsɛləˋreʃən]	n.	加速度
biomimetic	[baɪomɪˋmɛtɪk]	adj.	模擬生物特性的
dexterity	[dɛksˋtɛrətɪ]	n.	敏捷
kinematics	[ˌkɪnəˋmætɪks]	n.	動力學
iteration	[ˌɪtəˋreʃən]	n.	重複
velocity	[vəˋlɑsətɪ]	n.	速度、迅速
actuator	[`æktʃʊˌetə]	n.	促動器
microrobot	[`maɪkroˌrɑbɑt]	n.	微型機器人

設計類
1
建築類
2
科技類　醫療器材、
3
飯店、餐飲類
4
國貿類
5

A home robot is being unveiled in the Consumer Electronics Show (CES) in Las Vegas.

一台家用機器人在拉斯維加斯消費者電子展初次亮相。

I'm thrilled to unveil the incredibly cute robot, Kimmy, to all of you. It might look like a toy, with the height of 45 centimeters and weight of merely 4 kilograms, but it's a highly intelligent home robot. Once familiarized with its amicable attributes, users will become used to the presence of Kimmy as if it is a family member.

我很興奮能向各位揭幕這台非常可愛的家用機器人，Kimmy。它的高度是 45 公分，重量只有 4 公斤，看起來可能很像玩具，但是它是高度智能的家用機器人，一旦熟悉它友善的特性，使用者馬上會習慣 Kimmy 的存在，好像它是家人一般。

Kimmy is voice-controlled, and can individualize its sounds and tones in response to different family members, while showing various facial expressions on the rectangular screen, which serves as its head. Speaking of family

Kimmy 具備聲控功能，而且能因應不同家人個別調整它的聲音及語調，同時在這個矩形螢幕顯示各種表情，螢幕也是它的頭部。提到家人，Kimmy 能為了

members, Kimmy can calibrate for the needs of the elder, such as speaking at a louder volume, reminding them to take medicines and recording their blood pressures, etc.

The screen is also equipped with a camera, so it can be utilized as a surveillance camera when users are away from home. Kimmy also comes with wi-fi connectivity, a microphone, and 2 Bluetooth speakers. The built-in sensors allow it to avoid collision with people and objects.

長輩的需求做出校正，例如提高音量說話，提醒他們吃藥及記錄他們的血壓等等。

它的螢幕也配備相機，所以當使用者不在家時，它能當作監視器。Kimmy 也有 wi-fi 連接功能、一個麥克風及兩個藍芽喇叭。內建的感應器讓它避免碰撞到人和物體。

❶ The term cyborg originated from sci-fi novels.

❷ Cyborgs will become more and more prevalent.

❸ Machines have been used to assist patients with paralyzed limbs to restore their movement.

❹ Articulated robots can move with dexterity.

❺ Microrobots can be placed inside patients to assist doctors to make their diagnoses.

❻ The rapid development of A.I. might lead to the replacement of certain white-collar jobs.

❼ The research and development of home robots is becoming more and more urgent in an aging society.

❽ The application of robots in medical care will partially relieve medical professionals' burden.

① 半人半機械的機械人這一詞源自科幻小説。

② 機械人未來會越來越普遍。

③ 機械已經被用來協助肢體癱瘓的病人恢復行動能力。

④ 多關節機器人(articulated robots)能敏捷地行動。

⑤ 微型機器人能被放入病人體內協助醫生做出診斷。

⑥ 人工智慧急速發展,可能會導致某些白領階級的工作被取代。

⑦ 家用機器人的研發在老年化社會越來越迫切。

⑧ 機器人在醫療照護的應用將減輕醫護人員的部分負擔。

09

設計展

巴黎家具家飾展
Maison & Object in Paris

口譯專業字彙　基礎字彙

字彙	音標	詞性	中譯
multi-functional	[mʌltɪˋfʌŋkʃən!]	adj.	多功能的
polished	[ˋpɑlɪʃt]	adj.	拋光的
launch	[lɔntʃ]	v.	發行
cube	[kjub]	n.	立方體
interlocking	[ˌɪntəˋlɑkɪŋ]	adj.	連結的
staggered	[ˋstægəd]	adj.	交錯的
conceal	[kənˋsil]	v.	遮蔽
semicircular	[ˌsɛmɪˋsɚkjələ]	adj.	半圓形的
flip	[flɪp]	v.	翻轉
backrest	[ˋbækˌrɛst]	n.	靠背
extend	[ɪkˋstɛnd]	v.	延伸
upholster	[ʌpˋholstə]	v.	裝椅套
translucent	[trænsˋlusnt]	adj.	半透明的
adjustable	[əˋdʒʌstəb!]	adj.	可調整的
panel	[ˋpæn!]	n.	嵌板
pastel	[pæsˋtɛl]	n.	柔和色的

口譯專業字彙　進階字彙

字彙	音標	詞性	中譯
handcrafted	[`hænd͵kræftɪd]	adj.	手工製作的
mould	[mold]	n.	模具
monochrome	[`manə͵krom]	n., adj.	單色
plywood	[`plaɪ͵wʊd]	n.	夾板
cylindrical	[sɪ`lɪndrɪk!]	adj.	圓柱形的
sustainable	[ɑvaŋ`gɑrd]	adj.	永續的
aesthetic	[ɛs`θɛtɪk]	adj.	美學的
Baroque	[bə`rok]	n., adj.	巴洛克風格
dresser	[`drɛsə]	n.	衣櫥
mahogany	[mə`hagənɪ]	n.	桃花心木
cypress	[`saɪprɪs]	n.	檜木
copper	[`kapə]	n.	銅
oak	[ok]	n.	橡樹
ebony	[`ɛbənɪ]	n.	黑檀木
incised	[ɪn`saɪzd]	adj.	呈鋸齒狀的、雕刻的
highboy	[`haɪ͵bɔɪ]	n.	高腳抽屜櫃

A furniture designer is explaining the functions of a unique chair in Maison & Object in Paris.

一位家具設計師正在巴黎家具家飾展解釋一個獨特椅子的功能。

This multi-functional and multi-sided chair might seem avant-garde at first sight. It is made of staggered panels of pastel tones.

這個多功能及多邊椅子可能第一眼看來頗前衛。它以柔和色的嵌板互相交錯製作。

You might even feel a little puzzled regarding how to use it. What we have in mind for the design is to create a sustainable chair that caters to users of different age groups, and accompanies children as they grow up.

你甚至可能對如何使用感到有點困惑。我們設計時考慮的是創造一把能持續使用，迎合不同年齡的使用者，而且能陪伴小孩成長的椅子。

The chair is very lightweight and all of the edges are concealed by rubber strips for safety. As I speak, feel free to flip it -- you might be surprised by how

這個椅子很輕，而且為了安全，所有邊角都以橡膠條包覆。我一邊說，你們可以轉一下椅子─你可能會對它的多

versatile it is!

The panels are polished and of various shapes and sizes. The small circular one here can be used as a stool for young children, and the large semicircular one is for adults.

If you flip over and have the rectangular panel face upward, it serves as a side table or coffee table. As for the five short rectangular panels between the circular and semicircular ones, they serve as shelves.

功能感覺驚訝！

這些嵌板都經過拋光處理，有各種形狀和尺寸。這個小的圓形嵌板能當小朋友的凳子，大的半圓形嵌板可給成人使用。

如果你把它翻轉過來，讓長方形嵌板朝上，它能當邊桌或咖啡桌使用。至於圓形和半圓形嵌板之間的五片短的矩形嵌板則能當作架子。

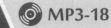
❶ These North European style sofas and armchairs are mainly minimalist.

❷ These pieces of Baroque furniture are filled with intricate sculptural details.

❸ Loft beds often go with desks or storage cabinets.

❹ Retractable storage cabinets are suitable for a variety of spaces.

❺ This highboy is made of mahogany.

❻ You can extend the sofa into a futon easily.

❼ Antique furniture made of ebony has become highly sought after by collectors in recent years.

❽ This folding wooden table is portable and easy to store.

❶ 這些北歐風的沙發和扶手椅以極簡風格為主。

❷ 這幾件巴洛克風格的家具充滿繁複的雕刻細節。

❸ 高架床常搭配書桌或收納櫃。

❹ 可伸縮的收納櫃適合各種空間。

❺ 這個高腳抽屜櫃由桃花心木製作。

❻ 您可以輕易地將這個沙發延伸成坐臥兩用床（futon）。

❼ 近年來對收藏家而言，以黑檀木製作的骨董家具變得炙手可熱。

❽ 這張折疊式的木製餐桌方便攜帶及收納。

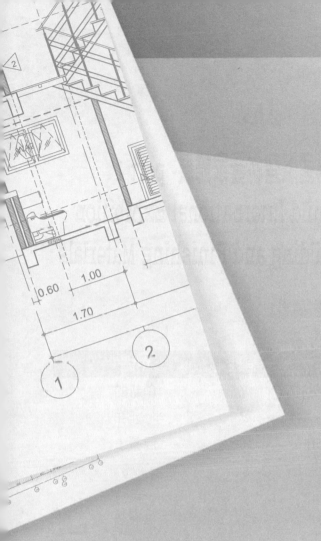

PART

建築類

篇章概述

建築類中，石材的英文字彙對許多讀者來說可能較不熟悉，可以多擴充這類別的語彙，在口譯時以更充分的表現應對。

10

建築展

莫斯科國際建材暨家飾展- part 1
Mosbuild International Exhibition
of Building and Finishing Materials

口譯專業字彙 　基礎字彙

字彙	音標	詞性	中譯
innovative	[`ɪnoˌvetɪv]	*adj.*	創新的
translucent	[træns`lusnt]	*adj.*	半透明的
concrete	[`kankrit]	*n.*	混凝土
tile	[taɪl]	*n.*	瓷磚
carbon	[`karbən]	*n.*	碳
optic	[`aptɪk]	*adj.*	光學的
fiber	[`faɪbɚ]	*n.*	纖維
insulation	[ˌɪnsə`leʃən]	*n.*	隔熱
confinement	[kən`faɪnmənt]	*n.*	限制
raise	[rez]	*v.*	提出、舉起
strand	[strænd]	*n.*	（線）一股
stability	[stə`bɪlətɪ]	*n.*	穩定
composite	[kəm`pazɪt]	*n.*	複合材料
acrylic	[æ`krɪlɪk]	*n., adj.*	壓克力
property	[`prapɚtɪ]	*n.*	屬性
flicker	[`flɪkɚ]	*v.*	閃耀

口譯專業字彙　進階字彙

字彙	音標	詞性	中譯
laminate	[`læmə‚net]	n.	層壓材料
marble	[`mɑrb!]	n.	大理石
quartz	[kwɔrts]	n.	石英
module	[`mɑdʒul]	n.	模塊
petrous	[`pɛtrəs]	adj.	岩石的
lime	[laɪm]	n.	石灰
granite	[`grænɪt]	n.	花崗岩
steel	[stil]	n.	鋼鐵
gravel	[`græv!]	n.	碎石
beech	[bitʃ]	n.	山毛櫸木材
oak	[ok]	n.	橡木
plaster	[`plæstɚ]	n.	灰泥
gypsum	[`dʒɪpsəm]	n.	石膏
cement	[sɪ`mɛnt]	n.	水泥
cementation	[‚simən`teʃən]	n.	水泥接合
balustrade	[‚bælə`stred]	n.	扶手

設計類

1

建築類

2

醫療器材、科技類

3

飯店、餐飲類

4

國貿類

5

A product development manager is giving a presentation on innovative building materials.

一位產品發展經理正在簡報創新建材。

Hello, everyone, welcome to the presentation on innovative building materials. I am going to introduce four materials, translucent concrete, smart tiles, carbon fiber and paper insulation, and there will be time for questions at the end of my presentation.

大家好，歡迎參與創新建材簡報。我將介紹四種建材，透光水泥、智慧瓷磚、碳纖維和紙絕緣體。簡報結束會有提問時間。

First, have you ever felt pressured by the confinement of concrete walls? Or have you hoped that there is more natural lighting in your residence? Well, translucent concrete has been commercialized to offer solutions to the problems I just raised. As the word "translucent" suggests,

首先，你是否曾經感到水泥牆的壓迫感？或你曾希望住宅有比較多的自然採光？嗯，透光水泥已被商品化，可以對剛剛我的問題做出解決。就像透光這個字暗示的，光能穿透用這種水泥製作的牆。它能透

light will shine through walls made of this kind of concrete. It is translucent because glass fiber strands are integrated into the material, and don't worry about the issue of stability. The glass fiber strands account for only four percent of the composite.

The next material I'd like to talk about is smart tiles. Smart tiles serve both safety and decoration purposes. Just like the first material, the unique property of smart tiles is based on the variation of concrete composite. The concrete of these tiles is mixed with acrylic fiber-optic channels, and the tiles flicker following your footsteps.

光因為玻璃纖維被融入這種建材。別擔心穩定性的問題。玻璃纖維只佔這複合材料的百分之四。

下一個我想討論的是智慧瓷磚。智慧瓷磚有安全及裝飾的目的。就像第一種建材，智慧瓷磚的特質是依據水泥複合材料的變化。這些瓷磚的水泥和壓克力光纖通道混合，會隨著你的步伐閃爍。

設計類
1
建築類
2
醫療器材、科技類
3
飯店、餐飲類
4
國貿類
5

❶ I will introduce 3 building materials.

❷ There will be time for questions after the intermission.

❸ These building materials include quartz, marble, and granite.

❹ Translucent concrete can increase natural lighting.

❺ Smart tiles do not require electricity.

❻ Smart tiles can also be applied to ceilings.

❼ The smart tiles on ceilings can produce the effect of the starry sky.

❽ Insulation materials on the roof help decrease energy consumption.

① 我將介紹三種建材。

② 中場休息之後會有提問時間。

③ 這些建材包括石英岩，大理石和花崗岩。

④ 透光水泥能增加自然採光。

⑤ 智慧瓷磚不須用電。

⑥ 智慧瓷磚也能應用於天花板。

⑦ 天花板的智慧瓷磚能製造星空般的效果。

⑧ 屋頂的隔熱材料能協助減少能源消耗。

11

建築展

莫斯科國際建材暨家飾展- part 2
Mosbuild International Exhibition
of Building and Finishing Materials

口譯專業字彙　基礎字彙

字彙	音標	詞性	中譯
contemporary	[kən`tɛmpə͵rɛrɪ]	adj.	當代的
construction	[kən`strʌkʃən]	n.	建設
predict	[prɪ`dɪkt]	v.	預測
residence	[`rɛzədəns]	n.	住宅
prevalent	[`prɛvələnt]	adj.	盛行的
literal	[`lɪtərəl]	adj.	照字面的
specifically	[spɪ`sɪfɪk!ɪ]	adv.	明確地
mold	[mold]	n., v.	鑄模、塑造
deem	[dim]	v.	認為
dramatic	[drə`mætɪk]	adj.	戲劇性的
climatic	[klaɪ`mætɪk]	adj.	氣候的
resistance	[rɪ`zɪstəns]	n.	抗性
retardance	[rɪ`tɑrdəns]	n.	延遲性
recycled	[rɪ`saɪk!d]	adj.	回收的
hazard	[`hæzə-d]	n.	危害
advantage	[əd`væntɪdʒ]	n.	優點

口譯專業字彙　進階字彙

字彙	音標	詞性	中譯
beam	[bim]	n.	橫樑
aggregate	[`ægrɪˌget]	n.	聚合體
mortar	[`mɔrtɚ]	n.	灰漿
plasticity	[plæs`tɪsətɪ]	n.	可塑性
adhesion	[əd`hiʒən]	n.	黏著
ferrous	[`fɛrəs]	adj.	含鐵的
elasticity	[ɪˌlæs`tɪsətɪ]	n.	彈性
ductility	[dʌk`tɪlətɪ]	n.	延展性
brittleness	[`brɪt!nɪs]	n.	脆性
malleability	[ˌmælɪə`bɪlətɪ]	n.	（金屬的）可塑性
compression	[kəm`prɛʃən]	n.	壓縮
silica	[`sɪlɪkə]	n.	矽土
reinforce	[ˌriɪn`fɔrs]	v.	加強
slate	[slet]	n.	石板
slab	[slæb]	n.	（木材的）板皮
glaze	[glez]	v.	上釉

設計類 1

建築類 2

醫療器材、科技類 3

飯店、餐飲類 4

國貿類 5

A product development manager is conducting the second part of the presentation on innovative building materials.

一位產品研發經理正在進行創新建材簡報的第二部分。

Now, let's move on to the next two materials, carbon fiber and paper insulation, which have been used in contemporary construction, and certainly will become much more prevalent.

接下來我將介紹的兩種建材是碳纖維和紙絕緣體。當代建築已經在使用這些建材，可肯定的是未來會更加普遍。

These materials have been predicted to be used widely in future construction, whether it's in office buildings or residences. The first one is carbon fibers, which you might be more familiar with than the other one.

這些建材被預測是未來建設都會廣泛使用的建材，不管是在辦公大樓或住宅。第一種是碳纖維，你們可能對這種比對另一種更熟悉。

Carbon fibers are flexible, lightweight, and extremely strong. Because of these qualities,

碳纖維有彈性、輕量而且極端強韌。因為這些特質，碳纖維容易塑

carbon fibers are easily molded, and thus deemed as the perfect material in regions affected by dramatic climatic changes, for instance, regions with typhoons and tornados.

Now, I'd like to move on to the second material, paper insulation. As you might have guessed from the literal meaning, it refers to the kind of material made from paper, more specifically, recycled paper. The advantages include insect resistance and fire retardance. Most importantly, it causes no health hazard.

形，因此在受極端氣候影響的區域，被視為是完美的建材，例如在有颱風和龍捲風的地區。

現在我想繼續介紹第二種建材，紙絕緣體。你們從字面的意思大概已經猜到，它是指以紙類，更精準來說，以資源回收紙類製作的建材。優點包括防蟲和阻燃性。最重要的是，它不會導致對健康的危害。

設計類

1

建築類

2

醫療器材、科技類

3

飯店、餐飲類

4

國貿類

5

❶ Paper insulation does not contain any chemical substances.

❷ Construction methods are adjusted according to different climates.

❸ One of the features of carbon fibers is plasticity.

❹ The process of housing construction generates a large amount of greenhouse gas.

❺ Paper insulation is a highly environmentally friendly building material.

❻ This picture shows how paper insulation is used in walls.

❼ Beams and timbers reinforce the stability of this house.

❽ Carbon fibers are even sturdier than steel.

❶ 紙絕緣體不含化學物質。

❷ 建設方式會隨不同的氣候調整。

❸ 碳纖維的特色之一是可塑性。

❹ 住宅建設的過程會產生大量的溫室氣體。

❺ 紙絕緣體是高度環保的建材。

❻ 這張圖片可看到紙絕緣體用在牆壁。

❼ 橫梁及棟木加強這棟房子的穩定性。

❽ 碳纖維甚至比鋼鐵強韌。

12

建築展

上海國際智能家居展覽會 Shanghai Smart Home Technology

口譯專業字彙　基礎字彙

字彙	音標	詞性	中譯
encompass	[ɪn`kʌmpəs]	v.	包含
device	K[dɪ`vaɪs]	n.	裝置
crucial	[`kruʃəl]	adj.	重要的
gadget	[`gædʒɪt]	n.	小玩意兒
preference	[`prɛfərəns]	n.	偏好
adjust	[ə`dʒʌst]	v.	調整
whereby	[hwɛr`baɪ]	adv., conj.	藉以
intricate	[`ɪntrəkɪt]	adj.	複雜的
entity	[`ɛntətɪ]	n.	實體
scenario	[sɪ`nɛrɪ͵o]	n.	場景
automation	[͵ɔtə`meʃən]	n.	自動化
autonomous	[ɔ`tɑnəməs]	adj.	自主的
glimpse	[glɪmps]	n.	一瞥
surveillance	[sɚ`veləns]	n.	監看
interface	[`ɪntɚ͵fes]	n.	界面
implementation	[͵ɪmpləmɛn`teʃən]	n.	安裝啟用

口譯專業字彙　進階字彙

字彙	音標	詞性	中譯
gizmo	[ˋgɪzmo]	n.	小發明
domotics	[dəˋmatɪks]	n.	家庭自動化
coded	[ˋkodɪd]	adj.	編碼的
transmitter	[trænsˋmɪtɚ]	n.	發射器
receiver	[rɪˋsivɚ]	n.	接收器
numerical	[njuˋmɛrɪk!]	adj.	數值的
protocol	[ˋprotəˌkɑl]	n.	通訊協定
troubleshooting	[ˋtrʌb!ˌʃutɪŋ]	n.	疑難排解
functionality	[ˌfʌŋkʃəˋnælɪtɪ]	n.	功能性
cross-platform	[ˋkrɔsˌplætˌfɔrm]	n.	跨平臺
connectivity	[kəˋnɛktɪvəˌtɪ]	n.	網路連線
console	[ˋkɑnsol]	n.	操縱臺
thermostat	[ˋθɝməˌstæt]	n.	自動調溫器
customization	[ˌkʌstəmaɪˋzeʃən]	n.	客製化
configure	[kənˋfɪgɚ]	v.	配置
configuration	[kənˌfɪgjəˋreʃən]	n.	配置

A presenter is explaining how a smart home functions.

一位演講者正在解釋智慧屋如何運作。

While the connections between home security systems and your smart phones are not uncommon, smart homes will eventually encompass devices of all areas, and those devices will communicate with one another. They will help you manage your household, so you can focus more on crucial parts of your life.

住宅保全系統和你的智慧型手機連結已經很普遍，而未來智慧屋會涵蓋所有領域的裝置，那些裝置還會彼此溝通。它們會協助你管理好家裡，這樣你就能更專注在人生重要的部分。

Earlier when I said "devices of all areas", I mean areas from automatic temperature control to tiny gadgets, such as smart fridges that track your food and sensors in bins that detect the kinds of trash.

早些當我說所有領域的裝置，我是指從自動調溫到小器具，例如智慧冰箱能追蹤你的食物，和垃圾桶內的感應器能偵測垃圾的種類。

The more these devices talk to

這些裝置彼此溝通越

one another, the more they will understand your lifestyle and personal preference whereby they adjust their operations. With this intricate web of communication, your house will become a living entity that responds to your lifestyle.

Now let me walk you through a scenario, and you'll have a sense of home automation. Picture this: On your way home in a self-driving car on a scorching hot day, you give a voice command to your smartphone, demanding a home air conditioner to be switched on, and catch a glimpse of what your children are doing from the home surveillance app ....

多,它們越能理解你的生活型態及個人偏好,並依此調整它們的運作。有這個複雜的溝通網路,你的房子將變成能呼應你生活型態的生命體。

現在讓我描繪一個場景,你們就會有家庭自動化的概念。想像一下,在炎熱的夏天,你坐自動駕駛車回家的途中,你對智慧型手機下一個口語指令,要求打開冷氣,順便從監視 app 看一下你的孩子正在做甚麼……。

設計類
1
建築類
2
醫療器材、科技類
3
飯店、餐飲類
4
國貿類
5

1 People taking care of the elderly or the sick can be assisted by smart homes.

2 This wristband device is connected to the smart home.

3 Smart homes can track inhabitants' usage patterns.

4 Smart homes can adapt to their inhabitants.

5 Digital technologies are increasingly incorporated into architectural designs.

6 The console offers an interface for the control of all the automated devices in the household.

7 Residents can also interact with the house remotely.

8 You can use a wireless network to link a variety of devices more flexibly.

① 在家照顧老人或病人的人能從智慧屋獲得輔助。

② 這個手環裝置和智慧屋連結。

③ 智慧屋能追蹤住戶的使用模式。

④ 智慧屋能適應住戶。

⑤ 數位科技逐漸和建築設計融合。

⑥ 這操縱臺提供控制所有屋內自動化裝置的介面。

⑦ 住戶也能從遠端和房子互動。

⑧ 你能使用無線網絡更靈活地連結各種裝置。

設計類

1

建築類

2

醫療器材
科技類

3

飯店、
餐飲類

4

國貿類

5

13

建築展

德國建築設計展 German Architecture and Design Exhibition

口譯專業字彙 基礎字彙

字彙	音標	詞性	中譯
architect	[`ɑrkə͵tɛkt]	n.	建築師
illustrate	[`ɪləstret]	v.	闡述
biodesign	[͵baɪodɪ`zaɪn]	n.	仿生設計
obviously	[`ɑbvɪəslɪ]	adv.	明顯地
relatively	[`rɛlətɪvlɪ]	adv.	相對地
formation	[fɔr`meʃən]	n.	形成
compare	[kəm`pɛr]	v.	比較
probe	[prob]	v.	探索
refined	[rɪ`faɪnd]	adj.	細微的
brick	[brɪk]	n.	磚
synthesize	[`sɪnθə͵saɪz]	v.	合成
microorganism	[͵maɪkro`ɔrgən͵ɪzəm]	n.	微生物
mineral	[`mɪnərəl]	n.	礦物
solution	[sə`luʃən]	n.	溶劑
facilitate	[fə`sɪlə͵tet]	v.	促進
emit	[ɪ`mɪt]	v.	散發

口譯專業字彙　進階字彙

字彙	音標	詞性	中譯
timber	[`tɪmbɚ]	n.	棟木
microbe	[`maɪkrob]	n.	微生物
self-sustaining	[sɛlf sə`stenɪŋ]	adj.	自給的
biodegradable	[`baɪodɪˏgredəb!]	adj.	生物能分解的
biodegrade	[`baɪodɪˏgred]	v.	生物分解
self-renewing	[sɛlf rɪ`njuɪŋ]	adj.	自我修補的
self-strengthening	[sɛlf strɛŋθənɪŋ]	adj.	自我增強的
biocement	[ˏbaɪosɪ`mɛnt]	n.	生物水泥
asphalt	[`æsfɔlt]	n.	瀝青
replicate	[`rɛplɪˏket]	v.	複製
incorporate	[ɪn`kɔrpəˏret]	v.	使混合
infuse	[ɪn`fjuz]	v.	注入
bacteria	[bæk`tɪrɪə]	n.	細菌
synthetic	[sɪn`θɛtɪk]	adj.	合成的
integrate	[`ɪntəˏgret]	v.	整合
bioprinting	[`baɪoˏprɪntɪŋ]	n.	生物印刷

An architect is illustrating the latest design concept called biodesign.

What kind of image springs to your mind when you hear the word "biodesign"? Obviously, it is a design method that utilizes biological formation. Though it's a relatively new concept among architects in the west, in fact centuries ago, people in India already began using tree roots as bridges. It might take 10 to 15 years for root bridges to fully form their shapes, yet they might last hundreds of years, and thus a highly sustainable and environmentally friendly construction.

Compared with the root bridges, western architects are probing

一位建築師正在闡述仿生設計這個最新的設計觀念。

當你聽到仿生設計時，什麼樣的形象躍入腦海裡？明顯地，它是利用生物形塑的設計方法。雖然在西方建築圈是相當新的觀念，事實上幾個世紀前，印度人已經利用樹根形塑成橋梁。樹根橋可能得花十到十五年長成形狀，但是它們能維持數百年，因此是高度永續及環保的建設。

和樹根橋相比，西方建築師正在探索更細微的

into more refined ways to develop building materials. Imagine that instead of employing construction workers to build your house, your house will not only grow itself, but also adjust itself automatically in response to climatic changes.

I'm referring to bricks made from concrete synthesized with microorganisms. How do the bricks grow? A special mineral solution is mixed with the concrete to facilitate the microorganisms to grow and harden the concrete. During the growing process, the bricks emit no greenhouse gases, and can be shaped in response to weather conditions.

發展建材的方法。想像一下，與其雇用建築工人蓋房子，未來你的房子不但會自己成長，也會因應氣候變化自動調整。

我指的是以微生物複合水泥製作的磚塊，這些磚塊是如何成長？一種特殊的礦物質溶液和水泥混合，促進微生物成長並硬化水泥。在成長過程，磚塊不會排放溫室氣體，而且可因應天氣情況被塑形。

設計類

1

建築類

2

醫療器材、科技類

3

飯店、餐飲類

4

國貿類

5

❶ Architectural designs that used to be seen only in sci-fi movies will become real in the near future.

❷ For example, balconies will be equipped with aprons for drones.

❸ Or even building materials will not be manufactured in traditional ways.

❹ The latest trend of architectural design is biodesign.

❺ Biodesign also includes using biodegradable materials, for example, cornstalks.

❻ Some biodesign buildings utilize materials synthesized with microbes and traditional materials.

❼ Some biodesign materials can self-renew and self-strengthen.

❽ Of course, the biggest advantage is that biodesign materials cause no harm to the environment.

❶ 以往科幻電影裡才能看到的建築設計，不久的未來就會成真了。

❷ 例如，陽台將配備有無人機的停機坪。

❸ 或是連建材都不再以傳統的方式生產。

❹ 建築設計的最新趨勢是仿生設計。

❺ 仿生設計也包括運用可生物分解的材料，例如，穀類的稈。

❻ 有的仿生設計的建築是使用微生物和傳統建材合成的建材。

❼ 有些仿生建材能自我修補及自我增強。

❽ 當然，仿生建材最大的優點是對環境無害。

14

建築展

台灣國際建築及空間設計展 Taiwan International Architecture and Space Design Expo

口譯專業字彙　基礎字彙

字彙	音標	詞性	中譯
exposition	[ˌɛkspəˋzɪʃən]	n.	博覽會
curator	[kjʊˋretɚ]	n.	館長、策展人
brief	[brif]	adj., n.	簡短的、簡報
decorative	[ˋdɛkərətɪv]	adj.	裝飾性的
ceramic	[səˋræmɪk]	adj.	陶器的
sanitary	[ˋsænəˌtɛrɪ]	adj.	衛生的
forum	[ˋforəm]	n.	討論會
renowned	[rɪˋnaʊnd]	adj.	有名的
expertise	[ˌɛkspɚˋtiz]	n.	專業知識
insight	[ˋɪnˌsaɪt]	n.	洞察力
keynote	[ˋkiˌnot]	n.	演說的主旨
finalize	[ˋfaɪn!ˌaɪz]	v.	完成
incorporate	[ɪnˋkɔrpəˌret]	v.	包含、使合併
innovative	[ˋɪnəˌvetɪv]	adj.	創新的
essential	[ɪˋsɛnʃəl]	adj.	必要的
sustainability	[səˌstenəˋbɪlətɪ]	n.	永續性

口譯專業字彙　　進階字彙

字彙	音標	詞性	中譯
emcee	[`ɛm`si]	*n.*	司儀
staging	[`stedʒɪŋ]	*n.*	舞台架設
logistics	[lə`dʒɪstɪks]	*n.*	物流、後勤
venue	[`vɛnju]	*n.*	活動、地點
demonstrate	[`dɛmən,stret]	*v.*	展示
portfolio	[port`folɪ,o]	*n.*	投資組合
segment	[`sɛgmənt]	*n.*	部分、區塊
domestic	[də`mɛstɪk]	*adj.*	國內的
follow-up	[`fɑlo`ʌp]	*n.*	後續動作
goodwill	[`gʊd`wɪl]	*n.*	商譽
contract	[`kɑntrækt]	*n.*	合約
headquarters	[`hɛd`kwɔrtɚz]	*n.*	總部
incentive	[ɪn`sɛntɪv]	*n.*	誘因
representative	[rɛprɪ`zɛntətɪv]	*adj., n.*	代表性的、代表人士
consensus	[kən`sɛnsəs]	*n.*	共識
alternative	[ɔl`tɚnətɪv]	*n.*	替代方案

設計類

1

建築類

2

醫療器材、
科技類

3

飯店、
餐飲類

4

國貿類

5

The curator of Taiwan International Architecture and Space Design Expo is giving a brief on the sections of the expo.

台灣國際建築與空間設計展的策展人正在簡報展區的類別。

Ladies and gentlemen, I'm honored to present an overview of the expo, and please feel free to interrupt me anytime if any question arises. The expo is divided into 5 sections: green building, smart home, decorative artwork, ceramic sanitary ware, and avant-garde lifestyle forum.

先生與女士，我很榮幸能呈現這場展覽的簡報。如果有任何問題，請隨時提出。這場展覽分為五個區塊：綠建築、智慧屋、家飾藝品、陶瓷衛浴設備及前衛生活型態論壇。

The forum section is a new addition this year, and not open to the public. In the forum section, we will invite several world-renowned architects to share their expertise and insights. You can find the names of the keynote speakers in the

論壇區是今年新加入的部分，且不對外開放。在論壇區，我們將邀請世界知名的建築師來分享他們的專業知識及見解。你們可以在企劃書裡找到主講人的名字，雖然這個名單不是最終

proposal, though the list is not finalized. As I have mentioned, this is the first time we incorporate a forum into the expo. It's also highly anticipated.

As for the green building and smart home sections, participants will have access to the most innovative technologies and essential construction materials for high-performance sustainability.

In total, the expo will feature over 150 architectural firms from Taiwan and around the world, as well as over 80 companies in the fields of decorative artworks and ceramic sanitary wares.

定案。如同我提過的，這是第一次我們在此展覽加入論壇，也備受期待。

至於綠建築和智慧屋區，參與者將能接觸到最先進的科技及能達到高績效永續目標的必備建築材料。

此次展覽共有 150 家以上來自台灣及世界各地的建築師事務所參與，以及 80 家以上家飾藝品和陶瓷衛浴設備領域的公司。

❶ I am honored to give you a brief on the participating companies in this exposition.

❷ This exposition is divided into 8 sections.

❸ 50 domestic companies will participate in this exposition.

❹ There are 120 overseas companies.

❺ The themes of the sections include basic building materials, innovative building materials, and smart homes, etc.

❻ The Innovative Building Material Section is mainly about the materials that go with smart homes.

❼ Visitors will obtain the latest information on sustainable building materials in the Green Building Section.

❽ Our team provides logistics consultancy.

① 很榮幸向各位簡報這次博覽會的參與廠商。

② 這次博覽會分為八個展區。

③ 這次博覽會有 50 家國內廠商參與。

④ 國外廠商則有 120 家。

⑤ 展區的主題包括基本建材、創新建材及智慧屋等等。

⑥ 創新建材區主要是關於能和智慧屋搭配的建材。

⑦ 訪客在綠建築區能取得關於永續建材的最新資訊。

⑧ 我們的團隊提供後勤諮詢。

15

建築展

建商商品介紹會
Builders' Merchandise Fair

口譯專業字彙 基礎字彙

字彙	音標	詞性	中譯
module	[`mɑdʒul]	n.	模塊
modular	[`mɑdʒələ]	adj.	模塊化的
cost-effective	[kɔst ɪ`fɛktɪv]]	adj.	成本效益的
time-saving	[`taɪm‚sevɪŋ]	adj.	省時的
relocatable	[‚rɪlo`ketəb!]]	adj.	可遷移的
sectional	[`sɛkʃən!]	adj.	區塊的
prefabricated	[‚pri`fæbrɪketɪd]	adj.	預製構件的
estimate	[`ɛstə‚met]	v.	預估
transportation	[‚trænspə`teʃən]	n.	運輸
off-site	[‚ɔf saɪt]	adj.	現場外的
assembly	[ə`sɛmblɪ]	n.	組裝
volumetric	[‚vɑljə`mɛtrɪk]	adj.	容積的
residential	[‚rɛzə`dɛnʃəl]	adj.	住宅的
stack	[stæk]	v., n.	堆疊
slab	[slæb]	n.	厚板
customization	[‚kʌstəmaɪ`zeʃən]	n.	客製化

口譯專業字彙　進階字彙

字彙	音標	詞性	中譯
versatile	[ˋvɝsət!]	adj.	靈活的、多功能的
layout	[ˋleˏaʊt]	n.	規劃圖
prestressed	[ˏprɪˋstrɛst]	adj.	預應力的
column	[ˋkɑləm]	n.	圓柱
soffit	[ˋsafɪt]	n.	下楣
cornice	[ˋkɔrnɪs]	n.	飛簷
arch	[artʃ]	n.	拱狀
precast	[prɪˋkæst]	adj.	預鑄的
cladding	[ˋklædɪŋ]	n.	覆面
infiltration	[ˏɪnfɪlˋtreʃən]	n.	滲透
erect	[ɪˋrɛkt]	v.	豎立
cellular	[ˋsɛljʊlɚ]	adj.	單元式製造的
casting	[ˋkæstɪŋ]	n.	鑄件
joist	[dʒɔɪst]	n.	桁樑
gypsum	[ˋdʒɪpsəm]	n.	石膏
accelerate	[ækˋsɛləˏret]	v.	加速

設計類 1

建築類 2

醫療器材、科技類 3

飯店、餐飲類 4

國貿類 5

A manager from a construction company is talking about the advantages of modular construction.

一位建設公司的經理正在討論模塊化建設的優點。

Good morning. I'm glad to talk to you about the unique service our company provides. As you already know, we specialize in modular construction. Why is it better to choose modular construction instead of traditional construction? Let me give you three reasons. The first is cost-effective, the second is time-saving, and the third is relocatable.

早安。很高興能跟你們談談我們公司獨特的服務。如同你們已經知道的，我們專精於模塊化建設。為什麼選擇模塊化建設比傳統建設好？讓我舉三個理由。第一是有成本效益，第二是省時，第三是可遷移。

How does it differ from traditional construction? Think about the way you build houses with Lego bricks. That's the basic idea behind modular construction,

模塊化建設和傳統建設有何不同?想一下你用樂高積木的磚塊蓋房子的方式。那就是模塊化建設的基本概念，類似

which is similar to building with Lego bricks.

Almost every section of your future house is prefabricated off-site in a factory, and it is estimated that up to 95% of modules are complete by the time of transportation. Because of rapid assembly, modular construction can save at least 50% of work days.

The units we produce in factories are called 3D volumetric modules. Later I'll show you the pictures of a variety of 3D volumetric modules, which we have utilized to build schools, residential houses, and commercial buildings.

用樂高積木蓋房子。

幾乎每個你未來房子的區塊都是在工廠生產編製，具估計高達 95% 的模塊在運輸前已經完成。因為能快速組裝，模塊化建設能節省至少 50%的工作天。

我們在工廠生產的單位稱為 3D 容積模塊。等一下會展示各種 3D 容積模塊和用這些模塊建築的學校，住宅和商業大樓的圖片。

設計類

1

建築類

2

醫療器材、科技類

3

飯店、餐飲類

4

國貿類

5

❶ Modular design can be applied to a wide range of areas.

❷ Modular design can also be applied to office furniture.

❸ Since most units are prefabricated in factories, the assembly process of modular construction does not generate lots of noise.

❹ Compared with traditional construction methods, modular construction offers more versatile methods.

❺ In fact, modular construction is more suitable for customization.

❻ Modules can be easily replaced during the assembly process.

❼ A room can be more simply added than in a traditional building process.

❽ Precast cladding panels can help control rain infiltration.

① 模塊化設計的應用範圍很廣。

② 模塊化設計也能應用至辦公室傢具。

③ 因為大部分單位都在工廠預製構件，模塊化建設的組裝過程不會產生太多噪音。

④ 和傳統建設比較，模塊化建設提供更靈活的方式。

⑤ 事實上，模塊化建設更適合客製化。

⑥ 在組裝過程中，可輕易更換模塊。

⑦ 比起傳統建造過程，加間房間更簡易。

⑧ 預鑄的護牆板能協助控制雨水滲透。

設計類

1

建築類

2

醫療器材、科技類

3

飯店、餐飲類

4

國貿類

5

16

建築展

華山文創園區綠建築展 Green Building Exhibition, Huashan Creative Park

口譯專業字彙　基礎字彙

字彙	音標	詞性	中譯
docent	[`dosnt]	n.	導覽員
concept	[`kansɛpt]	n.	觀念
misconception	[ˌmɪskən`sɛpʃən]	n.	誤解
involve	[ɪn`vɑlv]	v.	牽涉
compose	[kəm`poz]	v.	組成
device	[dɪ`vaɪs]	n.	裝置
element	[`ɛləmənt]	n.	元素
transform	[træns`fɔrm]	v.	轉變
residence	[`rɛzədəns]	n.	住宅
appliance	[ə`plaɪəns]	n.	電器
prime	[praɪm]	adj.	基本的、最佳的
install	[ɪn`stɔl]	v.	裝設
installation	[ˌɪnstə`leʃən]	n.	裝設
flow	[flo]	n.	水流
tap	[tæp]	n.	水龍頭
lavatory	[`lævəˌtorɪ]	n.	廁所

口譯專業字彙　　進階字彙

字彙	音標	詞性	中譯
restrictor	[rɪˋstrɪktə]	n.	限流器
sensor	[ˋsɛnsə]	n.	感應器
ventilation	[͵vɛnt!ˋeʃən]	n.	通風
solar	[ˋsolə]	adj.	太陽的
panel	[ˋpæn!]	n.	控電板
renewable	[rɪˋnjuəb!]	adj.	可更新的
conservation	[͵kɑnsəˋveʃən]	n.	保育
ecosystem	[ˋɛko͵sɪstəm]	n.	生態系統
cistern	[ˋsɪstən]	n.	貯水器
asbestos	[æsˋbɛstəs]	n.	石綿
geothermal	[͵dʒɪoˋθɝm!]	adj.	地熱的
insulated	[ˋɪnsjʊ͵letɪd]	adj.	隔熱的
ozone	[ˋozon]	n.	臭氧
organic	[ɔrˋgænɪk]	adj.	有機的
carbon footprint	[ˋkɑrbən ˋfʊt͵prɪnt]	adj. + n.	碳足跡
hydroelectric	[͵haɪdroɪˋlɛktrɪk]	adj.	水力發電的

設計類 1
建築類 2
科技類 醫療器材、 3
餐飲類 飯店、 4
國貿類 5

A docent working in the Green Building Exhibition in Huashan Creative Park is explaining the concept of green building to a group of visitors.

一位在華山文創園區綠建築展工作的導覽員正在向一群訪客解釋綠建築的概念。

Believe it or not, lots of people still have some misconceptions about green buildings. For example, some think the concept involves merely planting more trees around the house, while others view it as a system composed of expensive high-tech devices.

信不信由你，許多人對綠建築仍有一些誤解。例如，有些人以為這概念只牽涉到在房子周圍多種樹，而有些人將它視為由昂貴的高科技裝置組合成的一套系統。

Well, designing green buildings involves much more elements than the ones I just described.

嗯，設計綠建築牽涉到的元素比我剛剛描述的多很多。

Luckily, green buildings are quite affordable, and if you transform your residence into one, keep

幸運的是，綠建築蠻容易負擔得起。而且如果你計畫將住宅轉換成綠

these three ways in mind. First, begin with small steps to achieve sustainability. For instance, using energy efficient appliances and natural ventilation, as well as lighting.

Secondly, to save water, install flow restrictors and sensor taps in bathrooms. Such installation is already very common in public lavatories.

Another way to save water is to reduce water pressure. Thirdly, consider installing solar panels. Solar power is one of the prime renewable energies.

建築，記住這三個方式。首先，要達到永續目標，從小步驟做起。例如，使用節能家電及自然的空調系統及採光。

第二，為了達到省水的目標，在浴室裝設節水閥及自動感應水龍頭。這種裝置在公共廁所已經很普遍。

另一個省水的方式是減少水壓。第三，考慮裝設太陽能板。太陽能是最主要的可替代能源之一。

設計類

1

建築類

2

科技類 醫療器材、

3

餐飲類 飯店、

4

國貿類

5

❶ When designing green buildings, we must take the local climate into consideration.

❷ The structures of green buildings must be relevant to residents' lifestyles.

❸ Green roofs can achieve an insulation effect.

❹ Green walls can consume carbon dioxide.

❺ There are some creative ways to save water energy.

❻ For example, install cisterns.

❼ Do your best to recycle water used in the kitchen and bathroom.

❽ In tropical countries, solar panels should be promoted.

PART 2·建築展 16 —— 華山文創園區綠建築展
Green Building Exhibition, Huashan Creative Park

設計類

1

建築類

2

醫療器材·科技類

3

飯店·餐飲類

4

國貿類

5

❶ 設計綠建築時，要考慮當地的氣候。

❷ 綠建築的結構必須與住戶的生活型態有所關連。

❸ 綠化屋頂能達到隔熱效果。

❹ 植生牆能消耗二氧化碳。

❺ 有些有創意的方式能節省水資源。

❻ 例如，裝設儲水器。

❼ 盡量循環使用廚房及浴廁用水。

❽ 在熱帶國家，太陽能板應該加以推廣。

17

建築展

上海永續建築展
Shanghai Sustainable Building Expo

口譯專業字彙　基礎字彙

字彙	音標	詞性	中譯
interior	[ɪn`tɪrɪɚ]	adj., n.	內部的、內部
trend	[trɛnd]	n.	趨勢
arise	[ə`raɪz]	v.	形成、興起
awareness	[ə`wɛrnɪs]	n.	覺悟、意識
iconic	[aɪ`kɑnɪk]	adj.	代表性的
concrete	[`kɑnkrit]	n.	水泥
lush	[lʌʃ]	adj.	植被茂盛的
lushness	[lʌʃnɪs]	n.	蒼翠繁茂
proceed	[prə`sid]	v.	繼續進行
reduction	[rɪ`dʌkʃən]	n.	減少
artificially	[ˌɑrtə`fɪʃəlɪ]	adv.	人工地
sustain	[sə`sten]	v.	承擔
oxygen	[`ɑksədʒən]	n.	氧
generate	[`dʒɛnəˌret]	v.	產生
soil	[sɔɪl]	n.	土壤
curtain	[`kɝtn]	n.	窗簾

口譯專業字彙　進階字彙

字彙	音標	詞性	中譯
foliage	[`folɪɪdʒ]	n.	觀葉植物
irrigation	[ˌɪrəˋgeʃən]	n.	灌溉
atrium	[`atrɪəm]	n.	中庭
terrace	[`tɛrəs]	n.	露臺
refurnish	[rɪˋfɜˋnɪʃ]	v.	裝潢
restoration	[ˌrɛstəˋreʃən]	n.	整修
tier	[tɪr]	n.	層疊
vegetation	[ˌvɛdʒəˋteʃən]	n.	植被
module	[`madʒul]	n	模組、模塊
modular	[`madʒələ˞]	adj.	模件的
façade	[fəˋsad]	n.	建築物正面
vertical	[`vɜˋtɪkl̩]	adj.	垂直的
circulate	[`sɜˋkjəˌlet]	v.	循環
insulate	[`ɪnsəˌlet]	v.	絕緣、隔熱
emission	[ɪˋmɪʃən]	n.	排放
consumption	[kənˋsʌmpʃən]	n.	消耗

An architect is giving a presentation on green walls.

一位建築師正在介紹植生牆。

While organic architecture and minimalist interiors had taken center stage for decades in the last century, in the 1970s, a new trend of bringing nature into buildings arose. Some say it was a response to the growing awareness of environmental protection.

上個世紀，有機建築和極簡風的室內裝潢一直是數十年來的關注焦點，而在 1970 年代，興起一股將自然帶入建築的風潮。有些人說這風潮是呼應環保意識抬頭。

Regarding this trend, I'll focus on the green wall, one of the most iconic structures which attempt to turn a concrete jungle into natural lushness.

關於這股風潮，我的重點放在植生牆，在嘗試將都市叢林轉變成自然蒼綠景觀的結構中，植生牆是最具代表性的結構。

Before I proceed, I just want to point out briefly that a green wall is not an essential part of a green

在我繼續報告前，我只是想簡短指出，植生牆並不是綠建築必要的一

PART 2・建築展 17 —— 上海永續建築展
Shanghai Sustainable Building Expo

設計類

1

建築類

2

醫療器材、
科技類

3

飯店、
餐飲類

4

國貿類

5

building, though it does help with the reduction of carbon dioxide and production of oxygen.

Basically, a green wall is a wall artificially covered with foliage sustained by its own soil and irrigation system.

Now the picture you see Is the green wall In the atrium of Best Shopping Mall in Taichung, Taiwan. This green wall is 20 meters high, and looks just like a long lush curtain. It is estimated that the whole vegetation can generate 150 kilograms of oxygen every day.

部分，雖然它的確能幫助減少二氧化碳及製造氧氣。

基本上，植生牆是以人工方式將觀葉植物覆蓋其上，這些植物依賴的是專屬的土壤和灌溉系統。

現在你們看到的圖片是位於台灣台中貝斯特購物中心中庭的植生牆。這面牆高二十公尺，看起來就像蒼綠的長窗簾。據估計這一整片植被每天能生產 150 公斤的氧氣。

❶ Green walls can add lushness to the busy commercial district.

❷ Architects must design the irrigation system carefully.

❸ The major value of the green wall is to generate oxygen.

❹ Green walls indoors carry the function to purify air.

❺ The slide shows a green wall in Chicago, U.S.A.

❻ The façade of this building is covered with vegetation.

❼ The vegetation includes three tiers.

❽ To some degree, green walls can generate the insulation effect.

❶ 植生牆能為繁忙的商業區添加綠意。

❷ 建築師必須縝密地設計灌溉系統。

❸ 植生牆主要價值是能產生氧氣

❹ 室內的植生牆有淨化空氣的功能。

❺ 這張幻燈片顯示的是位於美國芝加哥的一面植生牆。

❻ 這棟建築物的正面被植被覆蓋。

❼ 這片植被共包括三個層次。

❽ 某種程度上，植生牆能產生隔熱效果。

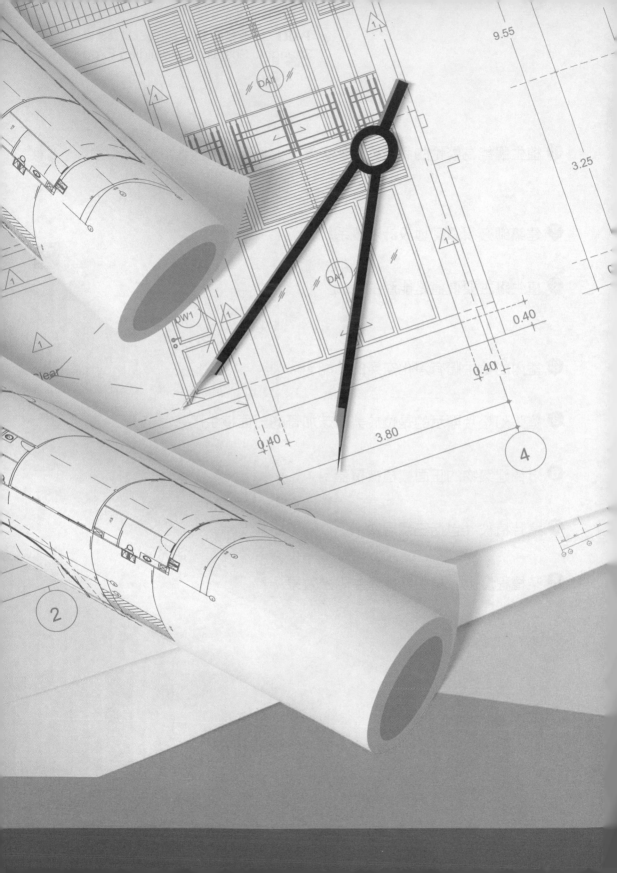

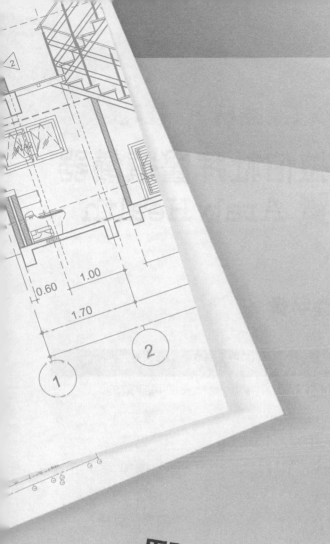

PART ③

醫療器材、科技類

篇章概述

醫療器材類的字彙可能對護理或醫學相關科系的學生來說較為熟悉，讀者可以先熟習這類字彙再做練習。除了口譯之外，從事醫療或科技業的也會常碰到這些字喔!

18

醫療器材、科技展

阿拉伯杜拜醫療儀器展覽 Arab Health

口譯專業字彙　基礎字彙

字彙	音標	詞性	中譯
wearable	[`wɛrəb!]	adj.	可穿戴的
assistive	[ə`sɪstɪv]	adj.	輔助的
unveil	[ʌn`vel]	v.	揭露
enhance	[ɪn`hæns]	v.	增加
aging	[`edʒɪŋ]	adj.	老化的
aim	[em]	v., n.	瞄準、目標
fatigue	[fə`tig]	n.	疲勞
diamond shaped	[`daɪəmənd ʃept]	adj.	菱形的
embed	[ɪm`bɛd]	v.	內嵌
associate	[ə`soʃet]	v.	聯想
blend	[blɛnd]	v.	混合
rehabilitative	[ˌrɪhəbɪlə`tetɪv]	adj.	復健的
tone down	[ton daʊn]	v. phr.	降低
lumbar	[`lʌmbɚ]	adj.	腰部的
undergarment	[`ʌndɚˌgɑrmənt]	n.	貼身衣
elastic	[ɪ`læstɪk]	adj.	彈性的

口譯專業字彙　進階字彙

字彙	音標	詞性	中譯
bandage	[`bændɪdʒ]	*n.*	繃帶
catheter	[`kæθɪtɚ]	*n.*	導管
forceps	[`fɔrsəps]	*n.*	鑷子
curette	[kjʊ`rɛt]	*n.*	刮匙
pipette	[pɪ`pɛt]	*n.*	移液管
stethoscope	[`stɛθə͵skop]	*n.*	聽診器
stretcher	[`strɛtʃɚ]	*n.*	擔架
syringe	[`sɪrɪndʒ]	*n.*	注射器
tourniquet	[`tʊrnɪ͵kɪt]	*n.*	止血帶、壓脈器
brace	[bres]	*n.*	支架
cast	[kæst]	*n.*	固定用敷料
crutch	[krʌtʃ]	*n.*	腋杖
defibrillator	[dɪ`fɪbrəletɚ]	*n.*	電擊器
thermometer	[θɚ`mɑmətɚ]	*n.*	溫度計
splint	[splɪnt]	*n.*	夾板
sling	[slɪŋ]	*n.*	懸帶

設計類 1

建築類 2

醫療器材、科技類 3

飯店、餐飲類 4

國貿類 5

A wearable assistive device for the elderly is being presented in Arab Health.

在阿拉伯杜拜醫療儀器展覽中,一項穿戴式輔具正在被介紹。

Ladies and gentlemen, I'm honored to unveil the amazing wearable assistive device that will greatly enhance the living quality of the aging population. This device aims to increase the muscle power so that daily movements, such as getting up, walking, and sitting down, don't generate fatigue on the wearer.

先生女士,很榮幸能發表這個很棒的穿戴式輔具,這個輔具將大幅改善老化人口的生活品質。這個輔具主要的目的是加強肌力,讓日常活動,如起身、走路和坐下,不會造成穿戴者的疲憊。

How does the device achieve that? Basically, these diamond shaped sensors are embedded with artificial intelligence technology that records the wearer's muscle movement, and adds strength when needed.

這要如何辦到呢?基本上,這些菱形的感應器有內嵌人工智慧科技,能記錄穿戴者的肌肉動作,並在需要時加強肌力。

At first glance, you might not associate this device with the lifestyle of assisted living.

That's exactly what our team had in mind when we designed this device. We hoped to design a device that blends in with everyday life, and tone down the rehabilitative look.

As you might have noticed, the one-piece clothing with sensors is very lightweight, and when the elderly put it on, the feel is not much different from wearing an undergarment. The clothing is made from elastic fabric, and in the lumbar area, there is a stronger band of fabric to offer extra support.

光看第一眼,你可能不會將這個輔具和照護生活型態聯想在一起。

那就是我們團隊當初在設計這輔具時,所考慮到的。我們希望設計出能融入日常生活的輔具,並讓復健商品的外觀看來柔和一些。

你可能注意到,這附帶感應器的一件式服裝非常輕,當長輩穿上時,感受跟穿內衣差不多。服裝是由彈性布料製作而成,在腰部的部分,有加強布料能提供額外支撐。

❶ The healthcare industry is a fast-growing industry.

❷ Assistive devices help improve the daily life of the aging population or physically and mentally challenged.

❸ Assistive devices can facilitate their independent movement.

❹ The trend of designing assistive and medical devices is to integrate advanced technologies.

❺ A company has developed a device that allows people to run bio-sample tests by themselves.

❻ This device will transmit test results to doctors via Bluetooth.

❼ A specific APP can keep track of test results.

❽ Medical professionals can monitor patients' health via the cloud.

設計類

1

建築類

2

醫療器材、科技類

3

飯店、餐飲類

4

國貿類

5

❶ 醫療保健產業是個快速成長的產業。

❷ 輔具能輔助改善老化人口或身心障礙者的日常生活。

❸ 輔具能促進他們獨立行動。

❹ 設計輔具和醫療儀器的趨勢是融入高科技。

❺ 有一間公司已經研發出讓民眾能自行測試生物檢體的裝置。

❻ 這個裝置會透過藍芽將測試結果傳送給醫生。

❼ 特定 APP 能追蹤測試結果。

❽ 醫護人員能透過雲端監督病人的健康。

19

醫療器材、科技展

台灣國際銀髮族暨健康照護產業展
Taiwan International Senior Lifestyle and Health Care Show

口譯專業字彙　基礎字彙

字彙	音標	詞性	中譯
population	[ˌpɑpjəˋlɛʃən]	n.	人口
reveal	[rɪˋvil]	v.	揭露
foldable	[ˋfoldəb!]	adj.	可摺疊的
foldability	[ˌfoldəˋbɪlətɪ]	n.	摺疊
sleek	[slik]	adj.	優雅的、線條流暢的
stylish	[ˋstaɪlɪʃ]	adj.	時髦的
composite	[kəmˋpɑzɪt]	adj.	複合的
Turkish	[ˋtɝkɪʃ]	n., adj.	土耳其語、土耳其的
flamboyant	[flæmˋbɔɪənt]	adj.	豔麗的
compartment	[kəmˋpɑrtmənt]	n.	隔間
detachable	[dɪˋtætʃəb!]	adj.	可拆卸的
tech-savvy	[tɛk ˋsævɪ]	adj.	精通科技的
equip	[ɪˋkwɪp]	v.	配備
record	[rɪˋkɔrd]	v.	紀錄
mild	[maɪld]	adj.	輕微的
dementia	[dɪˋmɛnʃɪə]	n.	失智

口譯專業字彙　進階字彙

字彙	音標	詞性	中譯
incubator	[ˋɪnkjəˌbetɚ]	n.	恆溫器
sphygmomanometer	[ˌsfɪgmoməˋnamətɚ]	n.	血壓計
gurney	[ˋgɝnɪ]	n.	推送病人的輪床
tongue depressor	[tʌŋ dɪˋprɛsɚ]	n.	壓舌板
gauze	[gɔz]	n.	紗布
suction	[ˋsʌkʃən]	n.	抽吸
otoscope	[ˋotəˌskop]	n.	耳鏡
resuscitator	[rɪˋsʌsəˌtetɚ]	n.	人工呼吸器
oxygen cylinder	[ˋaksədʒən ˋsɪlɪndɚ]	n.	氧氣瓶
laryngoscope	[ləˋrɪŋgəˌskop]	n.	喉鏡
tranquilizer	[ˋtræŋkwɪˌlaɪzɚ]	n.	鎮定劑
injection	[ɪnˋdʒɛkʃən]	n.	注射
antiseptic	[ˌæntəˋsɛptɪk]	adj., n.	抗菌的、抗菌劑
hypodermic	[ˌhaɪpəˋdɝmɪk]	adj., n.	皮下的、皮下注射器
ventilator	[ˋvɛnt!ˌetɚ]	n.	通風機
vial	[ˋvaɪəl]	n.	藥水瓶

The scooters for the elderly are being unveiled.

針對高齡人口的摩托車初次上市。

We are all aware that the aging population will account for most of the populations in many developed countries. Therefore, our company aims to develop products that promote the living quality for the elderly.

我們都知道在許多已開發國家，老化人口將佔一大部分。因此我們公司致力於研發提升老年人口生活品質的產品。

Today I am proud to reveal the latest series of foldable three wheel electric scooters. Don't they look sleek and stylish? You're welcome to try riding it, folding it, and carrying it around just to see how lightweight it is.

今天我很驕傲能發表最新系列的可折疊三輪電動小型摩托車。它們看來是不是很流線又時髦？歡迎大家試騎，折疊並拿拿看，感受一下它有多輕。

These scooters are not only foldable, but also colorful. Foldability is crucial so that those living in apartment complexes

這些小型摩托車不只能折疊，也有多樣色彩。能折疊是重要的，這樣公寓的住戶才能輕易移

can move & store these scooters without difficulty. Currently, they come in Turkish blue, flamboyant red, and lush green.

Besides, they are composite; the compartment at the front is detachable. When the user does not need the compartment, he can remove it easily.

Also, he does not need to be tech-savvy to operate the scooter. The scooter is equipped with A.I. technology to record the user's regular paths to assist users with mild dementia.

動並收納摩托車。目前，這系列有土耳其藍、烈焰紅和深綠色。

此外，這系列是複合式的摩托車；前方的置物箱是可以拆卸的。當使用者不需要置物箱時，他能輕易將它卸除。

而且，使用者不用精通科技也會操作，這產品配備有人工智慧科技，會記錄使用者常走的路徑，能協助有輕微失智症的使用者。

❶ As the population ages, the products that cater to seniors are gradually forming a huge industry.

❷ Daily goods required in the assisted lifestyle are different from those in the healthy lifestyle.

❸ A. I. technologies can help ensure the safety of patients with dementia.

❹ For example, when patients with mild dementia go out, the portable device can track their routes.

❺ If patients stray too far away from their daily routes, the device will automatically send a signal to their main caretakers.

❻ Proper assistive devices can help relieve the burden on caretakers.

❼ Long-distance care will become more prevalent.

❽ This exhibition also includes equipment that prevents accidents.

PART 3・醫療器材、科技展 19 — 台灣國際銀髮族暨健康照護產業展
Taiwan International Senior Lifestyle and Health Care Show

設計類

1

建築類

2

醫療器材、科技類

3

飯店、餐飲類

4

國貿類

5

❶ 隨著人口老化，針對銀髮族的產品漸漸形成龐大產業。

❷ 照護生活型態所需的日常用品和健康的生活型態不同。

❸ 人工智慧科技能協助確保失智症患者的安全。

❹ 例如，輕微的失智症患者外出時，這個隨身攜帶的裝置能追蹤他們的路徑。

❺ 若患者離開日常的路徑太遠，這個裝置能自動發送信號給主要的看護者。

❻ 適當的輔具能減輕照護者的負擔。

❼ 遠距照護在未來會更加普遍。

❽ 這次展覽也包括意外預防設備。

20

醫療器材、科技展

中國醫療器械展
China Medical Equipment Fair

口譯專業字彙　基礎字彙

字彙	音標	詞性	中譯
alternative	[ɔl`tɝnətɪv]	adj.	另類的
electroacupuncture	[ɪˌlɛktrə`pʌŋktʃɚ]	n.	電針
chiropractor	[`kaɪrəˌpræktɚ]	n.	脊骨神經醫師
electrode	[ɪ`lɛktrod]	n.	電極
pad	[pæd]	n.	襯墊
bionic	[baɪ`ɑnɪk]	adj.	仿生學的
pulse	[pʌls]	n.	脈搏
acupuncture	[ˌækjʊ`pʌŋktʃɚ]	v., n.	針灸
reusable	[ri`juzəb!]	adj.	可重複使用的
adhesive	[əd`hisɪv]	adj.	有黏性的
intensity	[ɪn`tɛnsətɪ]	n.	強度
waveform	[`wevˌfɔrm]	n.	波形
readout	[`ridˌaʊt]	n.	讀出
accessory	[æk`sɛsərɪ]	n.	配件
adaptor	[ə`dæptɚ]	n.	轉接器、變壓器
manual	[`mænjʊəl]	n.	手冊

口譯專業字彙 　進階字彙

字彙	音標	詞性	中譯
probe	[prob]	n.	探針
scalpel	[`skælpəl]	n.	解剖刀
dosage	[`dosɪdʒ]	n.	劑量
endoscope	[`ɛndə͵skop]	n.	內視鏡
anesthetic	[͵ænəs`θɛtɪk]	n.	麻醉劑
diagnose	[`daɪəgnoz]	v.	診斷
diagnosis	[͵daɪəg`nosɪs]	n.	診斷
rehabilitate	[͵rihə`bɪlə͵tet]	v.	復健
rehabilitation	[͵rihə͵bɪlə`teʃən]	n.	復健
laboratory	[`læbrə͵torɪ]	n.	實驗室
therapist	[`θɛrəpɪst]	n.	治療師
otolaryngology	[͵otə͵lærɪŋ`galədʒɪ]	n.	耳鼻喉科
ophthalmology	[͵afθæl`malədʒɪ]	n.	眼科
cardiology	[͵kardɪ`alədʒɪ]	n.	心臟科
cardiovascular	[͵kardɪo`væskjʊlɚ]	adj.	心血管的
orthopedics	[͵ɔrθə`pidɪks]	n.	骨科

A sales representative from an electroacupuncture machine manufacturer is describing his company's new product.

一位電針機製造商的業務代表正在描述他公司的新產品。

Hello, welcome to our product launch. I am very excited to tell you all about this electroacupuncture machine. Once considered a treatment in alternative medicine, electroacupuncture has received wider recognition by chiropractors and physical therapists in recent years. The new model I'm presenting has several features.

大家好，歡迎來我們的產品發表會。我很興奮向你們介紹這台電針機。電針機曾被視為另類醫療療法，電針機近年來已受到脊骨神經醫師和物理治療師的認可。現正發表的機型有幾個特色。

First, this machine was designed with bionic and microcomputer control technologies, so electric pulses can reach deeper muscle groups. The whole set includes

首先，這台機器以仿生學和微電腦控制科技設計，所以電脈衝能到達更深層的肌肉群。整組機器包括一個穴位偵測

an acupuncture point locater and stimulator, as well as 10 pairs of reusable and self-adhesive electrode pads, and thus it can be used with either needles or electrode pads.

Moreover, it is equipped with 6 output channels, which can be adjusted independently regarding intensities and waveforms; the intensities range from low, medium to high, and it provides 5 waveforms. The intensity and waveforms are shown on the 2 LCD screens, with readout function and an emergency stop button. The other accessories include an A/C adaptor, wires with alligator clips, and a user manual.

器及刺激器,及十對可重覆黏貼使用的電極片,因此這台機器能使用電針或電極片。

此外,它配備有六個輸出通道,每個通道能個別調整強度和波形。強度範圍從低度、中度至高度,並有五種波形。強度和波形在兩個 LCD 螢幕顯示,有讀出功能及緊急停止按鈕。其他配件包括 A/C 變壓器、鱷魚夾傳輸線及使用手冊。

1 First aid kits are commonly found medical devices in most families.

2 First aid equipment includes sphygmomanometers, thermometers, gauze, bandages, etc.

3 Consumers can monitor their health independently by using some medical devices.

4 Common assistance devices include hearing aids, dentures, crutches, wheelchairs, etc.

5 Electroacupuncture treatment is based on the theory of stimulation of acupuncture points.

6 Electroacupuncture treatment is a part of rehabilitative therapy.

7 China Medical Equipment Fair exhibits electronics, first aid equipment, and outsourcing services.

8 This exhibition also encompasses endoscopes, ultrasonic equipment, CT, MRI, etc.

❶ 急救箱是大部分家庭都有的醫療設備。

❷ 急救設備包括血壓計、溫度計、紗布和繃帶等。

❸ 消費者可使用一些醫療裝置自主監控健康。

❹ 常見的輔具包含助聽器、假牙、腋杖、輪椅等。

❺ 電針療法是依據對穴位刺激的原理。

❻ 電針療法是復健治療的一部分。

❼ 中國醫療器械展展出電子儀器、急救器材及外包服務。

❽ 此次展覽亦涵蓋內視鏡、超音波、電腦斷層掃描（Computed Tomography，CT）、和核磁共振造影（Magnetic Resonance Imaging，MRI）等儀器。

21

醫療器材、科技展

新加坡未來醫療博覽會 Singapore FutureMed Expo

口譯專業字彙　基礎字彙

字彙	音標	詞性	中譯
characteristic	[ˌkærəktəˋrɪstɪk]	adj., n.	特色
innovative	[ˋɪnoˌvetɪv]	adj.	創新的
transform	[trænsˋfɔrm]	v.	轉換
unprecedented	[ʌnˋprɛsəˌdɛntɪd]	adj.	前所未有的
telehealth	[ˋtɛləˌhɛlθ]	n.	遠程醫療
remote	[rɪˋmot]	adj.	遠距的
wristband	[ˋrɪstˌbænd]	n.	手環
replicate	[ˋrɛplɪˌket]	v.	複製
replication	[ˌrɛpləˋkeʃən]	n.	複製
replica	[ˋrɛplɪkə]	n.	複製品
anatomy	[əˋnætəmɪ]	n.	解剖學
skull	[skʌl]	n.	頭骨
pelvis	[ˋpɛlvɪs]	n.	骨盆
vessel	[ˋvɛs!]	n.	血管
prosthesis	[ˋprɑsθɪsɪs]	n.	義肢
expose	[ɪkˋspoz]	v.	使接觸到

口譯專業字彙 　進階字彙

字彙	音標	詞性	中譯
endocrinology	[ˌɛndokrɪˋnalədʒɪ]	n.	內分泌學
metabolism	[mɛˋtæb!ˌɪzəm]	n.	新陳代謝
physiatrist	[ˌfɪzɪˋætrɪst]	n.	物理治療醫師
otolaryngology	[ˌotəˌlærɪŋˋgalədʒɪ]	n.	耳鼻喉科
pediatrician	[ˌpidɪəˋtrɪʃən]	n.	小兒科醫師
gastroenterology	[ˌgæstroˌɛntəˋralədʒɪ]	n.	腸胃科
dermatology	[ˌdɚməˋtalədʒɪ]	n.	皮膚科
nephrology	[nɪˋfralədʒɪ]	n.	腎臟科
rheumatology	[ˌruməˋtalədʒɪ]	n.	風濕病學
tracheotomy	[ˌtrekɪˋatəmɪ]	n.	氣管切開術
defibrillator	[ˌdɪˋfɪbrəletɚ]	n.	電擊器
traction	[ˋtrækʃən]	n.	牽引、收縮
ostomy	[ˋastəmɪ]	n.	造口術
denture	[ˋdɛntʃɚ]	n.	假牙
orthotics	[ɔrˋθatɪks]	n.	矯正學
electrocardiogram	[ɪˌlɛktroˋkardɪəˌgræm]	n.	心電圖

設計類

建築類

醫療器材、科技類

飯店、餐飲類

國貿類

The curator of Singapore FutureMed Expo is giving a brief on the characteristics of this expo.

新加坡未來醫療博覽會的策展人正在給一場關於博覽會特色的簡報。

Innovative technologies are transforming the medical devices and the relationships between medical professionals and patients at an unprecedented speed. I will focus on the two major characteristics of this expo, telehealth and the application of 3D printing.

創新科技正以前所未有的速度改變醫療器材及醫療專業人員和病人間的關係。我將著重在博覽會的兩項特色，遠程醫療和 3D 列印的應用。

First, telehealth involves employing telecommunication technologies to promote the communication between remote healthcare providers and patients. Currently, the most common devices include smart watches and wristbands that

首先，遠程醫療牽涉到以電信科技提升遠端醫護服務提供者和病人之間的溝通。目前最普遍的器材包括智慧型手錶和手環，能監測基本的生命跡象，例如心跳和血壓，並以無線方式傳

monitor basic vital signs, such as heartbeats and blood pressure, which are transmitted wirelessly to healthcare providers. The telehealth section also showcases the latest wearable sensors.

Besides, 3D printing allows medical facilities to produce more personalized medical devices. Since 3D printing can precisely replicate each patient's anatomy, no matter it's the skull, pelvis or blood vessels, doctors can work on replicas before surgery.

Another application is in the realm of medical education. Medical students will have more access to replicated human parts when doing their research.

送給醫護服務提供者。遠程醫療區也會展出最新的穿戴式感應器。

此外，3D 列印讓醫療機構能製造更個人化的醫療器材。因為 3D 列印能精準地複製每個病人的生理構造，不管是頭蓋骨，骨盆或血管。醫師能在手術前在複製品上操作。

另一項應用是在醫療教育領域。做研究時，醫學系學生將有更多管道取得人體複製品。

❶ The molds produced by 3D printing technologies will assist learning.

❷ The process of manufacturing prostheses will become more personalized.

❸ The future trend of medical care will be consumer-oriented.

❹ Another trend is preventive medicine.

❺ Medical devices at home allow consumers to manage their health autonomously.

❻ The Internet of things will influence telehealth technologies tremendously.

❼ Powder bed fusion is the most common technology applied on 3D printing medical devices.

❽ In this exhibition, you can be exposed to IVD and POCT equipment.

❶ 3D 列印科技製造的模具能協助學習。

❷ 義肢的製作過程將更個人化。

❸ 未來醫療照護的趨勢將是消費者導向。

❹ 另一個趨勢是預防醫療。

❺ 居家醫療器材讓消費者更自主地掌控健康。

❻ 物聯網將對遠程醫療科技產生重大影響。

❼ 粉體熔化成型技術（powder bed fusion）是最廣泛應用在 3D 列印醫療器材的科技。

❽ 在這次展覽你能接觸到體外診斷（In Vitro Diagnosis，IVD）及定點照護（Point of Care Testing，POCT）儀器。

設計類

1

建築類

2

醫療器材、科技類

3

飯店、餐飲類

4

國貿類

5

22

柏林消費電子展
IFA Berlin

口譯專業字彙　基礎字彙

字彙	音標	詞性	中譯
barrier	[`bærɪr]	n.	障礙
sync	[sɪŋk]	v., n.	同時發生
synchronize	[`sɪŋkrənaɪz]	v.	使同步
synchronization	[ˌsɪŋkrənɪ`zeʃən]	n.	同步化
translate	[træns`let]	v.	翻譯
instantaneously	[ˌɪnstən`tenɪəslɪ]	adv.	即刻
facilitate	[fə`sɪləˌtet]	v.	促進
existing	[ɪg`zɪstɪŋ]	adj.	現存的
earbud	[`ɪrˌbʌd]	n.	耳塞式耳機
handsfree	[`hændfri]	adj.	不須手操作的
interpreter	[ɪn`tɝprɪtɚ]	n.	口譯員
core	[kor]	n.	核心
gadget	[`gædʒɪt]	n.	小器具、小玩意兒
wireless	[`waɪrlɪs]	adj.	無線的
real-time	[`riəl ˌtaɪm]	adj.	即時的
nifty	[`nɪftɪ]	adj.	精巧的

口譯專業字彙　進階字彙

字彙	音標	詞性	中譯
speech-to-text	[spitʃ tu tɛkst]	n.	語音轉文字
recognition	[ˌrɛkəgˈnɪʃən]	n.	識別
simulate	[ˈsɪmjəˌlet]	v.	模擬
viable	[ˈvaɪəbl̩]	adj.	可實行的
standalone	[ˈstændəˌlon]	adj.	獨立式的
cellular	[ˈsɛljʊlɚ]	adj.	蜂巢式的
connectivity	[kəˈnɛktɪvəˌtɪ]	n.	（網路）連線
multilingual	[ˈmʌltɪˈlɪŋgwəl]	adj.	多語的
lingo	[ˈlɪŋgo]	n.	行話
convert	[kənˈvɝt]	v.	轉換
conversion	[kənˈvɝʃən]	n.	轉換
conjunction	[kənˈdʒʌŋkʃən]	n.	關聯
simultaneously	[saɪməlˈtenɪəslɪ]	adv.	同時地
toggle	[ˈtɑgl̩]	v., n.	切換
colloquial	[kəˈlokwɪəl]	adj.	口語的
colloquialism	[kəˈlokwɪəlɪzəm]	n.	方言用語

A translation device is being unveiled in a press conference.

一場記者會正在發佈一個翻譯裝置。

Many of you might be frequent business travelers, and we know language barriers can add to the stress of travelling in a foreign country. The wearable translation device named Sync Speech translates your sayings instantaneously, facilitating the communication among people who don't speak one another's language and helping reduce the stress for travelers.

你們很多人可能是頻繁的商務旅行者，而我們知道語言隔閡會增加在外國旅行的壓力。這個名為同步説的穿戴式翻譯裝置能立刻翻譯你説的話，促進不同語言者之間的溝通，並幫助減少旅行者的壓力。

You might wonder what is the difference between this device and those existing translation apps? Here's the major difference—the wireless smart earbuds that play the translation only a few seconds after the app

你們可能想知道這裝置和那些現存的翻譯 app 有什麼不同。主要不同就是這些無線智能耳塞式耳機，它們在 app 完成翻譯幾秒鐘之後播出翻譯，讓你的

finishes the translating process, will allow you to stay handsfree.

In other words, the earbuds function as your personal interpreter. At the core of the translation process is our app, which you need to download to your smartphones before using the earbuds.

Later, I'd like to invite two people speaking different languages from our audience to try these earbuds out. Currently, our app supports English, French, Spanish, and German, and we plan to add Japanese, Korean and Mandarin Chinese in the following months.

雙手能空出來。

也就是說，這些耳機能當作你的個人口譯員。翻譯過程的核心是我們的 app，在使用耳機前你需要先下載到智慧型手機。

待會我想邀請兩位說不同語言的觀眾來試用這些耳機。目前，我們的 app 支援英文、法文、西班牙文和德文，未來幾個月我們計畫加入日文、韓文和中文普通話。

❶ Not everyone has a smartphone.

❷ So some people still use standalone electronic translators.

❸ When travelling, smartphone users can rely on translation apps to facilitate communication.

❹ When people need to talk face-to-face for a longer period, the function of translation apps seems a little insufficient.

❺ The translation gadget keeps you from having to look at your cell phone all the time.

❻ A few seconds after a person finishes talking, the wireless earbuds play the translation results.

❼ The gadget can translate almost simultaneously.

❽ A few seconds later, the other person hears French from the earbuds.

① 不是每個人都有智慧型手機。

② 所以仍有人使用獨立式的電子翻譯機。

③ 智慧型手機的使用者旅行時能依賴翻譯 app 協助溝通。

④ 需要面對面進行比較久的交談時，翻譯 app 的功能略顯不足。

⑤ 這個翻譯小裝置能讓你不需要一直看手機。

⑥ 一方說完話幾秒後，這組無線耳機就會播出翻譯結果。

⑦ 這個小裝置幾乎能同步翻譯。

⑧ 幾秒後對方從耳機聽到的就是法文。

23

醫療器材、科技展

台灣國際太陽光電展覽會
Taiwan International Photovoltaic Exhibition

口譯專業字彙　　基礎字彙

字彙	音標	詞性	中譯
photovoltaic	[ˌfotovalˋteɪk]	adj.	光電的
futureproof	[ˋfjutʃɚˌpruf]	adj.	不會在未來被淘汰的
waterproof	[ˋwɔtɚˌpruf]	adj.	防水的
accompany	[əˋkʌmpənɪ]	v.	陪伴
compose	[kəmˋpoz]	v.	組合
internal	[ɪnˋtɚn!]	adj.	內在的、內建的
external	[ɪkˋstɚnəl]	adj.	外在的、外接的
virtually	[ˋvɚtʃʊəlɪ]	adv.	幾乎
slim	[slɪm]	adj.	輕薄的
charge	[tʃɑrdʒ]	v.	充電
efficient	[ɪˋfɪʃənt]	adj.	有效率的
adopt	[əˋdɑpt]	v.	採用
portability	[ˌportəˋbɪlətɪ]	n.	便攜性
built-in	[ˋbɪltˋɪn]	adj.	內建的
manufacturer	[ˌmænjəˋfæktʃərɚ]	n.	製造商
warranty	[ˋwɔrəntɪ]	n.	保固

口譯專業字彙　進階字彙

字彙	音標	詞性	中譯
conduction	[kən`dʌkʃən]	n.	熱傳導
convection	[kən`vɛkʃən]	n.	對流
inverter	[ɪn`vɝtɚ]	n.	變流器
adaptor	[ə`dæptɚ]	n.	轉接器
susceptor	[sə`sɛptɚ]	n.	感受器
substrate	[`sʌbstret]	n.	陶瓷基板
installer	[ɪn`stɔlɚ]	n.	安裝器、安裝員
harness	[`hɑrnɪs]	v.	利用
generator	[`dʒɛnəˌretɚ]	n.	發電器
convert	[kən`vɝt]	v.	轉換
voltage	[`voltɪdʒ]	n.	電壓
insolation	[ˌɪnsə`leʃən]	n.	日曬
leverage	[`lɛvərɪdʒ]	n., v.	槓桿作用、發揮功效
fusion	[`fjuʒən]	n.	熔解
radiate	[`redɪˌet]	v.	散發光熱
radiation	[ˌredɪ`eʃən]	n.	輻射

設計類

1

建築類

2

醫療器材、科技類

3

飯店、餐飲類

4

國貿類

5

A product development manager is introducing his company's latest product, a portable photovoltaic panel, in a press conference.

一位產品研發經理正在記者會中介紹他公司的最新產品，攜帶式光伏充電板。

Good morning, it is an honor to introduce this innovative product, which I'm holding in my hand. Have you noticed how slim and light it is? The size is about the same as that of an iPad, and weighs only 250 grams.

早安，很榮幸能介紹這創新的產品，就是我正拿在手裡的。你們有沒有發現它有多輕薄？它的尺寸和 iPad 差不多，重量只有 250 克。

This portable charger is designed to serve as back-up power on busy working days and relaxing leisure days.

這個攜帶式充電板設計的目的是能在繁忙的工作日及放鬆的休閒日當作備用電源。

It is basically composed of a 10 watt photovoltaic panel and an 10,000 mAh internal battery with dual built-in USB ports and 1

基本上，它是由一個 10 瓦特的光伏充電板和 10,000 毫安時的內建電池組合而成。有

USB-C port. Also, it's waterproof and shockproof.

兩個內建 USB 插孔和一個 USB-C 插孔。而且，它防水又防震。

Moreover, I'd like to emphasize that with the 10,000 mAh internal battery and 3 USB ports, virtually all USB compatible devices can be charged in a highly efficient way.

此外，我想強調 10,000 毫安時的內建電池及三個 USB 插孔能以高效率的方式將幾乎所有 USB 相容的裝置充電。

This charger is the first device in the green technology field to adopt a USB-C port, which is futureproof and allows your device to be charged at the maximum speed.

這個充電板是綠能科技業第一項採用 USB-C 插孔的產品，不會被未來淘汰，且裝置能以最快速度充電。

設計類

1

建築類

2

醫療器材、科技類

3

飯店、餐飲類

4

國貿類

5

❶ Solar energy is one of several important renewable energies.

❷ Numerous gadgets can leverage solar power.

❸ The products that utilize solar power are increasingly diversified.

❹ Wearable devices, for example, smart watches, can also adopt solar power.

❺ Rooftop solar panels help reduce enormous electric bills.

❻ It is an innovative practice to apply solar panels on vehicles.

❼ Photovoltaic cells are an important technology that harnesses solar energy.

❽ Solar energy is an inexhaustible energy.

❶ 太陽能是數種重要的可替代能源之一。

❷ 許多的小裝置能發揮太陽能的功效。

❸ 利用太陽能的產品越來越多樣化。

❹ 穿戴式裝置，例如智能手錶，也能採用太陽能。

❺ 屋頂的太陽能板幫助省下可觀的電費。

❻ 將太陽能板應用到交通工具是一項創新的用途。

❼ 光伏電池是一項利用太陽能的重要科技。

❽ 太陽能是取之不盡的能源。

24

医療器材、科技展

美國地熱能協會地熱能博覽會 GEA GeoExpo

口譯專業字彙　基礎字彙

字彙	音標	詞性	中譯
heat pump	[hit pʌmp]	n.	熱泵
conventional	[kən`vɛnʃən!]	adj.	慣例的
ventilation	[ˌvɛnt!`eʃən]	n.	空調設備
apparatus	[ˌæpə`retəs]	n.	儀器；設備
expose	[ɪk`spoz]	v.	暴露
vandalism	[`vændlɪzəm]	n.	破壞行為
negligible	[`nɛɡlɪdʒəb!]	adj.	微不足道的
maintenance	[`mentənəns]	n.	維修
durable	[`djʊrəb!]	adj.	耐用的
eco-friendly	[`ɪkɔˌfrɛndlɪ]	adj.	環保的
Fahrenheit	[`færənˌhaɪt]	n.	華氏的
Celsius	[`sɛlsɪəs]	n.	攝氏的
circulate	[`sɝkjəˌlet]	v.	循環
loop	[lup]	n.	迴圈
duct	[dʌkt]	n.	輸送
extract	[ɪk`strækt]	v., n.	提煉

口譯專業字彙　進階字彙

字彙	音標	詞性	中譯
compressor	[kəm`prɛsə]	n.	壓縮機
kilowatt	[`kɪlo͵wɑt]	n.	千瓦
combustion	[kəm`bʌstʃən]	n.	燃燒
emit	[ɪ`mɪt]	v.	散發
emission	[ɪ`mɪʃən]	n.	散發
polyethylene	[͵pɑlɪ`ɛθə͵lin]	n.	聚乙烯
conversion	[kən`vɝʃən]	n.	轉換
trench	[trɛntʃ]	v.	挖溝
refrigerant	[rɪ`frɪdʒərənt]	n.	冷媒
deplete	[dɪ`plit]	v.	耗盡
drill	[drɪl]	n., v.	鑽孔
reverse	[rɪ`vɝs]	v.	翻轉
absorb	[əb`sɔrb]	v.	吸收
emanate	[`ɛmə͵net]	v.	（氣體）散發
distribute	[dɪ`strɪbjʊt]	v.	分配
configuration	[kən͵fɪgjə`reʃən]	n.	配置

設計類 1

建築類 2

科技類 醫療器材、 3

餐飲類 飯店、 4

國貿類 5

A speaker at GEA GeoExpo is talking about the benefits of geothermal heat pumps.

美國地熱能協會地熱能博覽會的一位演講者正在談論地熱能熱泵的優點。

What are the main benefits of installing a geothermal heat pump? The first that comes to mind is the cost. Although it costs more for installation at the beginning, in the long run, it will decrease your ventilation bill by up to 30% or 40%.

安裝地熱能熱泵主要的優點有哪些？第一個想到的是成本。雖然最初安裝成本比較貴，長遠來看，熱泵能降低30%至40%的空調費用。

In fact, it is estimated that heat pumps use merely about one sixth of electricity compared with traditional heating and cooling systems.

事實上，據估計，和傳統的空調系統比較的話，熱泵只使用電量的六分之一。

The second advantage is its low maintenance. Since the apparatus is buried a few feet

第二個優點是少量維修。因為這裝置是埋在地底數英呎深，不會受

underground, it is not exposed to the effects of weather or vandalism. We might even say that the maintenance is negligible.

到天氣或人為破壞的影響。我們甚至能説只需要極少的維修。

In other words, geothermal heat pumps are extremely durable; according to some research, they can keep functioning effectively for 25 to 50 years.

也就是説，地熱能熱泵極端地耐用。根據一些研究，它們能持續有效率地運作長達 25 至 50 年。

On top of these advantages, it is also highly eco-friendly; no greenhouse gases are released during the operation. Besides, it generates little noise. In fact, the noise is as little as that of a refrigerator.

除了這些優點，熱泵非常地環保。運作中不會產生任何溫室氣體。此外，它運作時幾乎沒有噪音，事實上，音量和一台電冰箱的音量一樣低。

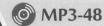
❶ The soil a few feet underground keeps a constant temperature of about 50 degrees Fahrenheit.

❷ The loop is a part of the basic structure of a geothermal heat pump.

❸ In winter, the duct system transmits heat throughout the house.

❹ In summer, the duct system sends heat to outdoors in the reversed direction.

❺ The loop configuration is installed vertically or horizontally.

❻ Geothermal heat pumps are considered the most eco-friendly and the most efficient ventilation systems.

❼ The loop are made up of polyethylene pipes.

❽ Horizontal loops are more common in residential areas.

❶ 地底數英呎之下，土壤保持華氏 50 度左右的恆溫。

❷ 迴圈是地熱能熱泵的基本構造的一部份。

❸ 冬天時，輸送管系統將熱能傳送到房子各處。

❹ 夏天時，輸送管系統以相反的方向將熱能傳送到室外。

❺ 迴圈配置分為垂直和水平兩種方向。

❻ 地熱能熱泵被視為最環保且最有效率的空調系統。

❼ 迴圈是由聚乙烯導管組合而成。

❽ 水平迴圈在住宅區較為普遍。

25

醫療器材、科技展

亞洲永續能源科技展 SETA (Sustainable Energy and Technology Asia)

口譯專業字彙　基礎字彙

字彙	音標	詞性	中譯
startup	[ˋstɑrtˏʌp]	n.	新興公司
address	[əˋdrɛs]	v., n.	致詞
backup	[ˋbækˏʌp]	v., n.	備用
yield	[jild]	v., n.	產生
pollutant	[pəˋlutənt]	n.	汙染物
off-peak	[ˋɔfˏpik]	adj.	非高峰的
utilize	[ˋjut!ˏaɪz]	v.	利用
hydrogen	[ˋhaɪdrədʒən]	n.	氫
store	[stor]	v.	儲存
storage	[ˋstorɪdʒ]	n.	儲存
popularize	[ˋpɑpjələˏraɪz]	v.	普及化
residential	[ˏrɛzəˋdɛnʃəl]	adj.	住宅的
aforementioned	[əˋforˋmɛnʃənd]	adj.	上述的
utility	[juˋtɪlətɪ]	n.	公用事業
theoretically	[ˏθɪəˋrɛtɪk!ɪ]	adv.	理論地
self-sufficient	[sɛlf səˋfɪʃənt]	adj.	自給的

口譯專業字彙　進階字彙

字彙	音標	詞性	中譯
redistribute	[ˌridɪsˋtrɪbjʊt]	v.	重新分配
ozone	[ˋozon]	n.	臭氧
off-grid	[ɔf ˋgrɪd]	adj.	電力自給的
configure	[kənˋfɪgɚ]	v.	配置
turbine	[ˋtɝbaɪn]	n.	渦輪機
blade	[bled]	n.	槳葉
hydropower	[ˋhaɪdroˌpaʊɚ]	n.	水力發電
offshore	[ˋɔfˋʃor]	n.	離岸的
tubular	[ˋtjubjɔlɚ]	adj.	管狀的
nacelle	[nəˋsɛl]	n.	吊艙
foundation	[faʊnˋdeʃən]	n.	地基
rotor	[ˋrotɚ]	n.	轉片
axis	[ˋæksɪs]	n.	軸
rotate	[ˋrotet]	v.	旋轉
rotation	[roˋteʃən]	n.	旋轉
generator	[ˋdʒɛnəˌretɚ]	n.	發電機

A speaker from a renewable energy startup is addressing the advantages of wind turbine generator and unveiling a new product.

With the rapid growth of wind farms all over the world since the 1980s, the advantages of wind turbine generators in terms of cost, environmental friendliness, and electricity yield have been widely proven. For instance, during operation, wind turbine generators emit no air pollutants.

Moreover, in areas with stable wind, the energy source is unlimited, and during off-peak seasons, electricity from wind farms can be utilized to produce hydrogen gas, which is then stored, further generating

一位替代能源新興公司的演講者正針對風力渦輪發電機的優點發表演說，並介紹一項新產品。

自從 1980 年代起，風力發電廠在世界各地快速興起，風力渦輪發電機的優點，如成本、環保及電力產量，已經被廣泛證實。例如，在運作過程中風力渦輪發電機不會散發任何氣體汙染物質。

此外，在風力穩定的地區，這種能源是取之不盡的，在非高峰期，風力發電廠產生的電力能被利用製造氫氣，將氫氣儲存後，需要時能再產生電力。

electricity when needed.

However, compared with solar panels, rooftop wind turbine generators have not been so popularized in residential areas. With the aforementioned advantages in mind, our company designed this small-scale wind turbine generator. We have overcome the major obstacle of rooftop wind turbines, that is, noise.

With these specifically designed blades, it is almost silent when functioning. Theoretically, combined with solar panels, the rooftop wind turbine would allow a household to be self-sufficient, off-grid.

然而，和太陽能板比較，屋頂型風力渦輪發電機在住宅區還不是很普及。考慮到上述優點，我們公司設計了這個小型風力渦輪發電機。我們已經克服屋頂型風力渦輪發電機主要的障礙，就是噪音。

有了這些特殊設計的葉片，它運作時幾乎是無聲的。理論上，和太陽能板一起使用時，屋頂型風力渦輪發電機能讓一戶家庭的電力完全自給。

❶ Wind farms generate a large amount of renewable energy.

❷ When wind power is not sufficient, backup power is needed.

❸ Backup power is provided by solar cells or hydropower.

❹ The major wind turbine generators include horizontal axis wind turbines and vertical axis wind turbines.

❺ Offshore wind farms are a global trend.

❻ Wind turbine generators are composed of a nacelle, a tower, blades, and a generator, etc.

❼ Among renewable energies, wind power is the most competitive economically.

❽ Wind turbine generators do not generate radiation during operation.

❶ 風力發電廠生產大量的可替代能源。

❷ 當風能量不夠時，必須使用備用電源。

❸ 備用電源可由太陽能電池或水力發電提供。

❹ 主要的風力渦輪發電機包括水平軸風力機與垂直軸風力機。

❺ 離岸式風力發電廠是全球的趨勢。

❻ 風力渦輪發電機是由吊艙、塔架、葉片和發電機等組合而成。

❼ 風力在可替代能源中是最具經濟競爭性的。

❽ 風力渦輪發電機運作中不會產生輻射。

26

醫療器材、科技展

台灣國際綠色產業展
Taiwan International Green Industry Show

口譯專業字彙　基礎字彙

字彙	音標	詞性	中譯
power strip	[`pauɚ strɪp]	n.	延長線
cost-effective	[kɔst ɪ`fɛktɪv]	adj.	有成本效益的
hassle-free	[`hæs! fri]	adj.	沒有麻煩的
conserve	[kən`sɝv]	v.	節約
plug	[plʌg]	n., v.	插頭、接通電源
socket	[`sakɪt]	n.	插座
surge	[sɝdʒ]	v.	激增
electronics	[ɪlɛk`tranɪks]	n.	電子儀器、電子學
circuit	[`sɝkɪt]	n.	電路
conduit	[`kandʊɪt]	n.	導線管
customizable	[`kʌstəmˌaɪzəb!]]	adj.	可訂做的
reprogram	[rɪ`progræm]	v.	重新設定
designate	[`dɛzɪgˌnet]	v.	指定
constant	[`kanstənt]	adj.	持續的
charge	[tʃardʒ]	v.	充電
cable	[`keb!]	n.	電纜、連接線

口譯專業字彙 進階字彙

字彙	音標	詞性	中譯
specification	[͵spɛsəfə`keʃən]	n.	規格
transformer	[træns`fɔrmə]	n.	變壓器
combustion	[kəm`bʌstʃən]	n.	燃燒
protector	[prə`tɛktə]	n.	保護裝置
carbon footprint	[`kɑrbən fʊt͵prɪnt]	n.	碳足跡
consumption	[kən`sʌmpʃən]	n.	消耗
watt	[wɑt]	n.	瓦特
detector	[dɪ`tɛktə]	n.	偵測器
infrared	[ɪntrə`rɛd]	n.	紅外線
circuitry	[`sɝkɪtrɪ]	n.	電路系統
gasohol	[`gæsəhɔl]	n.	汽油醇
biomass energy	[`baɪo͵mæs `ɛnədʒɪ]	n.	生物質能
biofuel	[`baɪo͵fjʊəl]	n.	生質燃料
biodiesel	[`baɪo͵dizḷ]	n.	生化柴油
inverter	[ɪn`vɝtə]	n.	變流器
methane	[`mɛθen]	n.	甲烷

設計類

1

建築類

2

科技類 醫療器材、

3

餐飲類 飯店、

4

國貿類

5

A sales representative is introducing a smart power strip.

一位業務代表正在介紹智慧型延長線。

Hello, I am excited to tell you all about this smart power strip.

嗨，我很高興能向你們介紹這個智慧型延長線。

Using a smart power strip is your first step towards building a smart home, and it is probably the most cost-effective and hassle-free device, especially for those who live in crowded apartments where the installation of large scale renewable energy devices, such as solar panels and wind turbines, is simply impossible.

使用智慧型延長線是你建構智慧住宅的第一步驟，而且它很可能是成本效益最高，也最不麻煩的裝置，尤其對住在擁擠公寓的人而言，裝設大型替代能源裝置是不可能的，例如太陽能板和風力渦輪。

A smart power strip disables phantom energy automatically, thus reducing electricity bills. By phantom energy, I'm referring to

智慧型延長線能自動消除耗電的狀況，因此能減少電費。我是指電器關掉後，插頭仍插著所

the electricity that's kept drawn after electronic appliances are turned off, but still plugged in.

造成的耗電。

Our power strip comes with built-in Wi-Fi connectivity, and with our app, you can monitor and control any appliance anytime, anywhere on your smartphone.

我們的智慧型延長線配備 Wi-Fi 連線，利用我們的 app，你能用智慧型手機隨時隨地監控電器的使用狀態。

As you might have noticed, the power strip has eight sockets in total: four standard sockets, two USB sockets and two always-on sockets. Particularly, the surge protector will protect your electronics by cutting off the circuit in case of power surge.

你們可能已經注意到，這延長線共有八個插座四個插座：四個標準插座、兩個 USB 插座和兩個不斷電插座。尤其，當電壓遽增時，電湧保護器會切斷電路，保護你的電器。

1 Unmanned vehicles have been applied in the fields of monitoring environment, exploring terrain, and maintaining solar panels.

2 The smart power strip has a lifespan of up to 15 years, and is thus worth investing in.

3 This smart power strip is equipped with a motion detector.

4 When no movement is detected, the power strip turns off the outlets.

5 Users can set the timer on a motion-detecting power strip regarding when to shut off.

6 With the Wi-Fi smart power strip, you can look up the power consumption on the exclusive app.

7 "Reducing carbon footprint" is the theme of this expo.

8 The highlights of this expo include low-carbon transportation, energy policy making, and green industry.

❶ 無人載具已被應用至環境監測、地形探勘、太陽能板維護等領域。

❷ 智慧型延長線的使用年限高達十五年，因此值得投資。

❸ 這個智慧型延長線配備有動態偵測器。

❹ 沒有偵測到動作時，延長線會關閉插座。

❺ 使用者可以用動態偵測延長線上的計時器設定關閉時間。

❻ 使用配有 Wi-Fi 的智慧型延長線，你能在專屬 app 查詢耗電量。

❼ 減少碳足跡是這次博覽會的主題。

❽ 這次博覽會的重點包括低碳運輸、能源決策及綠能產業。

27

醫療器材、科技展

東京車展 Tokyo Motor Show

口譯專業字彙　基礎字彙

字彙	音標	詞性	中譯
fuel cell	[`fjʊəl sɛl]	n.	燃料電池
stunning	[`stʌnɪŋ]	adj.	令人驚豔的
metallic	[mə`tælɪk]	adj.	金屬的
suede	[swed]	n.	絨面革
lining	[`laɪnɪŋ]	n.	內層
eye-catcher	[`aɪ͵kætʃɚ]	n.	引人注目的東西
showcase	[`ʃo͵kes]	v.	展示
combination	[͵kɑmbə`neʃən]	n.	結合
futuristic	[͵fjutʃɚ`ɪstɪk]	adj.	未來的
embody	[ɪm`bɑdɪ]	v.	體現
vapor	[`vepɚ]	n.	蒸汽
harness	[`hɑrnɪs]	v.	利用、駕馭
refuel	[rɪ`fjuəl]	v.	補給燃料
horsepower	[`hɔrs͵paʊɚ]	n.	馬力
tank	[tæŋk]	n.	槽
absolutely	[͵æbsə`lutlɪ]	adv.	絕對地

口譯專業字彙　進階字彙

字彙	音標	詞性	中譯
ion	[`aɪən]	*n.*	離子
anode	[`ænod]	*n.*	正極
cathode	[`kæθod]	*n.*	陰極
electrolyte	[ɪ`lɛktrəˌlaɪt]	*n.*	電解液
proton	[`protɑn]	*n.*	質子
atom	[`ætəm]	*n.*	原子
electrode	[ɪ`lɛktrod]	*n.*	電極
electrolysis	[ɪlɛk`trɑləsɪs]	*n.*	電解作用
alkali	[`ælkəˌlaɪ]	*n.*	鹼
catalyst	[`kætəlɪst]	*n.*	催化劑
membrane	[`mɛmbren]	*n.*	薄膜
combustion	[kəm`bʌstʃən]	*n.*	燃燒
thermodynamic	[ˌθɝ·modaɪ`næmɪk]	*adj.*	熱力學的
molecule	[`mɑləˌkjul]	*n.*	分子
polymer	[`pɑlɪmɚ]	*n.*	聚合物
methanol	[`mɛθəˌnol]	*n.*	甲醇

A product development manager is introducing a new fuel cell car.

一位產品研發經理正在介紹一台新的燃料電池汽車。

How exciting it is to unveil our latest hydrogen fuel cell car. This stunning car with the metallic silver exterior and suede lining interior is a sure eye-catcher. This car showcases the combination of futuristic style and the latest green technology.

真興奮能介紹我們最新的氫燃料電池汽車。這台令人驚豔的車有金屬銀的外觀及絨面革內裝，能吸引眾人目光。這台車展現了未來風格和最新綠能科技的結合。

Before I go into further details, let me talk a little about the theme of this show, eco-friendly innovation, which, in my opinion, is best embodied by the fuel cell.

在進入更多細節前，我想稍微談一下這次展覽的主題，環保創新，我認為燃料電池最能體現這個主題。

Fuel cells are absolutely clean power generators. By harnessing hydrogen, fuel cells can generate electricity almost endlessly, and

燃料電池是毫無汙染的發電機。藉由利用氫氣，燃料電池幾乎能無止盡地產生電力，而且

emit only vapor when functioning.

運作時只會產生水蒸氣。

A single tank of hydrogen can keep the car traveling up to 350 miles before it needs to be refueled.

一槽氫氣能讓這台車行駛達 350 英里，然後再補充氫能源。

Besides, it takes no more than 5 minutes to refuel. Our fuel cell engine delivers 130 horsepower.

此外，充滿氫能源的時間不到五分鐘。我們的燃料電池引擎能傳達 130 馬力。

We are also displaying the hydrogen generating station. In a few minutes, I will be more than glad to explain how it works if you have further questions.

我們也展出製氫站。幾分鐘後，如果你們有更多問題，我很樂意向你們解釋製氫站如何運作。

設計類

1

建築類

2

科技類 醫療器材、

3

餐飲類 飯店、

4

國貿類

5

❶ The engines of electric cars are very quiet without the noise of vibration.

❷ The interior of the car is adorned with sporty details.

❸ Simply put, fuel cells are hydrogen-burning power generators.

❹ Self-driving cars are the spotlights of this year's Tokyo Motor Show.

❺ Government incentives boosted the sales of electric cars.

❻ The fuel cell cars will be launched in China, followed by the launch in Japan.

❼ Hybrid cars have more ready markets in developed countries.

❽ More prevalent hybrid cars include gasoline-electric and diesel-electric hybrids.

❶ 電動車的引擎非常安靜，沒有震動的噪音。

❷ 這台車的內裝以運動風細節裝飾。

❸ 簡單來説，燃料電池就是燃燒氫氣的發電機。

❹ 自動駕駛車是今午東京車展的注目焦點。

❺ 政府的獎勵促進了電動車的銷售量。

❻ 這款燃料電池汽車會先在中國上市，接著在日本。

❼ 油電混合車在已開發國家有較多的現有市場。

❽ 較普遍的油電混合車包括石油電力混合車及柴油電力混合車。

28

醫療器材、科技展

國際食品加工及製藥機械展
International Food Processing & Pharmaceutical Machinery Show

口譯專業字彙　基礎字彙

字彙	音標	詞性	中譯
processing	[`prasɛs]	v.	加工
exhibitor	[ɪg`zɪbɪtɚ]	n.	參展者
pharmaceutical	[ˌfɑrmə`sjutɪk!]	adj.	藥物的
machinery	[mə`ʃɪnərɪ]	n.	機械
distinguished	[dɪ`stɪŋgwɪʃt]	adj.	卓越的
renowned	[rɪ`naʊnd]	adj.	知名的
pavilion	[pə`vɪljən]	n.	展館
hub	[hʌb]	n.	中樞
ceremony	[`sɛrəˌmonɪ]	n.	典禮
cutting-edge	[`kʌtɪŋ ɛdʒ]	adj.	最尖端的
spectrum	[`spɛktrəm]	n.	光譜、範圍
procure	[pro`kjʊr]	v.	獲得
booth	[buθ]	n.	攤位
packaging	[`pækɪdʒɪŋ]	n.	包裝
bakery	[`bekərɪ]	n.	麵包店
beverage	[`bɛvərɪdʒ]	n.	飲料

口譯專業字彙　進階字彙

字彙	音標	詞性	中譯
turnkey	[`tɝnˌki]	*adj.*	可立即使用的
temper	[`tɛmpɚ]	*v.*	調和
refrigeration	[rɪˌfrɪdʒəˈreʃən]	*n.*	冷藏
pulverize	[`pʌlvəˌraɪz]	*v.*	磨成粉
pulverizer	[`pʌlvəˌraɪzɚ]	*n.*	磨粉機
seal	[sil]	*v.*	密封
granulate	[`grænjəˌlet]	*v.*	使成粒狀
coater	[kotɚ]	*n.*	塗料器
assembly	[əˈsɛmblɪ]	*n.*	機械的裝配
label	[`leb!]	*v., n.*	貼標籤、標籤
milling	[`mɪlɪŋ]	*n.*	碾磨
extruder	[ɛkˈstrudɚ]	*n.*	擠壓機
grinder	[`graɪndɚ]	*n.*	研磨機
tumbler	[`tʌmblɚ]	*n.*	滾筒
injector	[ɪnˈdʒɛktɚ]	*n.*	注射器
valve	[vælv]	*n.*	閥

設計類

1

建築類

2

醫療器材、科技類

3

飯店、餐飲類

4

國貿類

5

A presenter is illustrating the highlights of International Food Processing and Pharmaceutical Machinery Show in the opening ceremony.

一位演講者正在開幕典禮中描述國際食品加工及製藥機械展的焦點。

Good morning, distinguished guests and media friends! Welcome to our show. The show is a hub for food processing and pharmaceutical machinery from all over the world. Buyers will have access to the machines of outstanding quality and cutting-edge designs. Certainly, from the wide spectrum of machines, they can procure the products of interest at the most competitive prices.

早安，各位嘉賓及媒體朋友們！歡迎來到這場展覽。這場展覽是來自世界各地食品加工及製藥機械的集中地。買家們能接觸到高品質及最尖端設計的機械。當然，從各種多樣化的機械中，買家們能以最具競爭性的價格購買到有興趣的產品。

In total, there are 284 exhibitors from 38 countries, and there are 5 pavilions, which are China, the

這次總共有來自 38 個國家的 284 家參展者，共有五個展館，分

USA, Latin American nations, Japan and Taiwan.

The food processing machinery includes packaging handling, meat tempering, vegetable processing, beverage preparation, refrigeration, and bakery equipment, as well as turnkey systems.

The pharmaceutical machinery ranges from processing, packaging, and laboratory equipment, which is further divided into detailed categories, such as pulverizer, drying machines, filling and sealing machines, coater, granulator, etc.

別是中國、美國、拉丁美洲國家、日本及台灣。

食品加工機械包括包裝處理、肉類處理、蔬菜加工、飲料製作、冷藏及烘培設備，也有啟鑰系統。

製藥機械則涵蓋加工、包裝及實驗設備，更細分為磨粉機、乾燥機、填充和密封機、塗料器、製粒機等等。

❶ The Taiwan Pavilion displays processing and packaging machinery of innovative designs.

❷ Intelligent machines echo the government's industrial transformation policy.

❸ The EU Pavilion is a new addition this year.

❹ It is estimated that the exhibition in the Taipei World Trade Center will accommodate at least 250 exhibitors.

❺ The booths in this exhibition amounted to 590.

❻ The number of participants this year surpassed that during the past years.

❼ Foreign manufacturers view this exhibition as the springboard to enter the Asian market.

❽ The multifaceted food culture in Taiwan has facilitated the progress of food processing industry.

❶ 台灣展館展示了創新設計的加工及包裝機械。

❷ 智慧型機械呼應了政府的產業轉型政策。

❸ 歐盟國家展館是今年新增加的展館。

❹ 預計在台北世貿中心的這次展覽，能容納至少 250 家參展者。

❺ 這次展覽的攤位多達 590 個。

❻ 今年參與者的數量超越以往。

❼ 外國廠商將這場展覽視為進入亞洲市場的跳板。

❽ 台灣多元的食品文化促進了食品加工業的進步。

29

醫療器材、科技展

亞太電子商務展
e-Commerce Expo Asia

口譯專業字彙　基礎字彙

字彙	音標	詞性	中譯
delineate	[dɪ`lɪnɪˌet]	v.	描述
bellwether	[`bɛlˌwɛðɚ]	n.	領頭羊、前導者
chain	[tʃen]	v., n.	鏈、連鎖
enterprise	[ɛntɚˌpraɪz]	n.	企業
retention	[rɪ`tɛnʃən]	n.	保留
seminar	[`sɛməˌnɑr]	n.	專題討論會
foster	[`fɔstɚ]	v.	促進
critical	[`krɪtɪkl]	adj.	關鍵的
fraud	[frɔd]	n.	詐騙
independent	[ˌɪndɪ`pɛndənt]	adj.	獨立的
reshape	[ri`ʃep]	v.	重新塑造
commerce	[`kɑmɚs]	n.	商業
analyze	[`ænlˌaɪz]	v.	分析
analysis	[ə`næləsɪs]	n.	分析
evaluate	[ɪ`væljʊˌet]	v.	估價
assess	[ə`sɛs]	v.	估算

口譯專業字彙　進階字彙

字彙	音標	詞性	中譯
escrow	[ˋɛskro]	n., v.	暫由第三方保管
token	[ˋtokən]	n.	代碼
tokenization	[ˌtokənaɪˋzeʃən]	n.	代碼化系統
cache	[kæʃ]	n.	快取記憶體
extranet	[ˋɛkstrənɛt]	n.	外聯網、商際網路
corroborate	[kəˋrabəˌret]	v.	證實、鞏固
precision	[prɪˋsɪʒən]	n.	精密度
spyware	[ˋspaɪˌwɛr]	n.	間諜軟體
ransomware	[ˋrɑnsəmˌwɛr]	n.	勒索軟體
encrypt	[ɛnˋkrɪpt]	v.	編碼
decrypt	[dɪˋkrɪpt]	v.	解碼
paradigm	[ˋpærəˌdaɪm]	n.	典範
integration	[ˌɪntəˋgreʃən]	n.	整合
miniaturization	[ˌmɪnɪətʃəraɪˋzeʃən]	n.	微型化
affiliation	[əˌfɪlɪˋeʃən]	n.	隸屬
pageview	[ˋpedʒˌvju]	n.	網頁瀏覽量

設計類
1
建築類
2
科技類　醫療器材、
3
餐飲類　飯店、
4
國貿類
5

A representative from the organizer of e-Commerce Expo Asia is delineating the highlights of the expo.

一位亞太電子商務展的籌備代表正在描述展覽焦點。

Good morning, honorable guests. This four-day expo is considered the bellwether among similar exhibitions.

各位嘉賓，早安。這場維期四天的展覽被視為類似展覽的前導者。

It offers comprehensive and cutting-edge solutions to all the sectors in e-commerce, including escrow service, customer service, customer retention, supply chain and logistics, digital and mobile marketing, etc.

對所有電子商務的區塊提供了全面且尖端的解決方案，包括信託付款服務、客服、客戶維繫、供應鏈及物流、數位及行動行銷等等。

The expo joins B2B and B2C buyers, sellers, distributers, and IT professionals.

這展覽集結了 B2B 和 B2C 買家、賣家、經銷商及 IT 產業專業人士。

It gathers 70 enterprises from six nations, ranging from social media and digital marketing companies to App developers, website designers, and e-commerce outsourcing companies.

The speakers in our seminars will share crucial insights on the hottest topics, such as anti-fraud solutions, big data analysis and applications, and how IoT (Internet of Things) will reshape e-commerce.

一共有來自六個國家的 70 個企業，包含社群媒體及數位行銷公司、App 研發者、網站設計師及電子商務外包公司。

研討會的講者將分享他們對最熱門話題的洞見，例如反詐騙解決方案、大數據分析及應用和物聯網如何重新塑造電子商務。

設計類

1

建築類

2

醫療器材、科技類

3

飯店、餐飲類

4

國貿類

5

❶ The seminars on the solutions to spyware and ransomware drew the most attendees.

❷ For startups and independent retailers, we recommend that they sign up for one-on-one consultation sessions.

❸ Free consultations from these e-commerce experts are a major appeal to visitors.

❹ The e-Commerce Expo is the best venue for startups to acquire all the know-how.

❺ B2C retailers from Taiwan will share their success stories.

❻ If consumers enter this discount code at checkout, they will receive a 15% discount.

❼ We need to consider user reviews when devising our marketing strategy.

❽ Third party payment platforms are highly developed in China.

設計類

1

建築類

2

科技類 醫療器材、

3

餐飲類 飯店、

4

國貿類

5

❶ 針對間諜軟體和勒索軟體的解決方案研討會吸引最多人出席。

❷ 對於新興公司和獨立零售商,我們建議他們報名一對一的諮商。

❸ 電子商務專家的免費諮商是主要吸引訪客的元素。

❹ 電子商務展對新興公司而言,是取得專業知識的最佳場合。

❺ 來自台灣的 B2C 零售商將分享他們的成功故事。

❻ 如果消費者在結帳時輸入這個折扣代碼,他們能有 85 折的折扣。

❼ 研發行銷策略時,我們需要考慮使用者評價。

❽ 中國的第三方支付平台非常發達。

30

醫療器材、科技展

半導體應用科普展
Semiconductor Application Exhibition

口譯專業字彙　基礎字彙

字彙	音標	詞性	中譯
semiconductor	[ˌsɛmɪkən`dʌktɚ]	n.	半導體
diode	[`daɪod]	n.	兩極管
apply	[ə`plaɪ]	v.	應用
application	[ˌæplə`keʃən]	n.	應用
sophisticated	[sə`fɪstɪˌketɪd]	adj.	精緻的
processor	[`prɑsɛsɚ]	n.	處理器
intend	[ɪn`tɛnd]	v.	打算
anode	[`ænod]	n.	正極
cathode	[`kæθod]	n.	陰極
current	[`kɝənt]	adj., n.	現在的、電流
switch	[swɪtʃ]	n.	電閘
abbreviation	[əˌbrivɪ`eʃən]	n.	縮寫
categorize	[`kætəgəˌraɪz]	v.	分類
discrete	[dɪ`skrit]	adj.	分離的
optoelectronics	[ˌɑptəˌɪlɛk`tranɪks]	n.	光電子學
precision	[prɪ`sɪʒən]	n.	精密

口譯專業字彙　進階字彙

字彙	音標	詞性	中譯
electron	[ɪˋlɛktrɑn]	n.	電子
conduction	[kənˋdʌkʃən]	n.	傳導
valence	[ˋveləns]	n.	原子價
conductivity	[ˌkɑndʌkˋtɪvətɪ]	n.	導電率
rectifier	[ˋrɛktəˌfaɪɚ]	n.	整流器
rectification	[ˌrɛktəfəˋkeʃən]	n.	整流
amplification	[ˌæmpləfəˋkeʃən]	n.	擴大、振幅
condenser	[kənˋdɛnsɚ]	n.	冷凝器，電容器
converter	[kənˋvɝtɚ]	n.	變流器
wafer	[ˋwefɚ]	n.	晶圓片
insulator	[ˋɪnsəˌletɚ]	n.	絕緣體
metrology	[mɪˋtrɑlədʒɪ]	n.	計量學
polycrystal	[ˌpɑlɪˋkrɪstl̩]	n.	多晶體
plasma	[ˋplæzəmə]	n.	電漿
transistor	[trænˋzɪstɚ]	n.	電晶體
thyristor	[θaɪˋrɪstɚ]	n.	閘流體

設計類

1

建築類

2

醫療器材、科技類

3

飯店、餐飲類

4

國貿類

5

A docent in the Semiconductor Application Exhibition in a science museum is talking to a group of students who intend to choose related science majors in the future.

科博館的導覽員正在半導體應用科普展對一群將來打算主修科學相關科系的學生講解。

You probably have heard that semiconductors are the core of most electronic appliances. Simply put, semiconductor devices function as switches that control the flow of a large amount of current, and they are categorized into discrete, integrated circuit, and optoelectronic devices.

你可能曾經聽過半導體是大部分電器的核心。簡單來說，半導體元件的功能是作為控制大量電流的電閘，而半導體元件被分類成分離式元件、積體電路與光電元件。

The most basic and widely used discrete semiconductor device is a diode. The current in a diode flows in only one direction, from the anode to the cathode. The

最基本也最廣泛使用的分離式半導體元件是兩極管。兩極管的電流只往一個方向，從正極到陰極。兩極管最普遍的

most common application of diodes is LEDs, which is the abbreviation of light emitting diodes.

The other devices that are made with semiconductors in daily life include CPUs, smartphones, televisions, digital cameras, and even rice cookers. Moreover, semiconductors are applied to sophisticated equipment that requires high-precision and ultra-speed, for example, military, laboratory and advanced medical care equipment.

應用是 LED，LED 是發光兩極管的縮寫。

其他應用半導體製造的裝置有 CPU、智慧型手機、電視、數位照相機，甚至電子鍋。此外，半導體被應用到需要高精準度及高速運轉的精密設備，例如軍隊設備、實驗室設備和高階醫療器材。

設計類

1

建築類

2

科技類 醫療器材、

3

餐飲類 飯店、

4

國貿類

5

❶ SEMICON Taiwan is considered the hub of the latest trends from relevant industries.

❷ Taiwan's semiconductor industry has a tremendous impact on the country's economy.

❸ SEMICON Southeast Asia showcased innovative technologies on smart manufacturing.

❹ Microelectronics industry continues to prosper due to the rise of IoT.

❺ The expo offers a great opportunity for networking.

❻ The expo encompassed nano technology and IC design sectors.

❼ SEMICON Southeast Asia plays a crucial role in the local industrial transformation.

❽ Forums on LED technology and sustainable manufacturing have been very well received by attendees.

設計類

1

建築類

2

科技類 醫療器材、

3

餐飲類 飯店、

4

國貿類

5

❶ 台灣國際半導體展被視為相關產業最新趨勢的中樞。

❷ 台灣的半導體產業對台灣的經濟有重大的影響。

❸ 東南亞國際半導體展展出智慧型製造的創新科技。

❹ 因為物聯網的興起,微電子產業持續繁榮。

❺ 這場展覽提供擴充人脈的絕佳機會。

❻ 這場展覽包含奈米科技區和 IC 設計區。

❼ 東南亞國際半導體展在當地的產業轉型扮演重要的角色。

❽ 與會者對 LED 科技論壇和永續製造論壇的反應都不錯。

31

日本國際穿戴式裝置科技展 Wearable Device & Technology Expo

口譯專業字彙　　基礎字彙

字彙	音標	詞性	中譯
virtual	[ˋvɝtʃʊəl]	adj.	虛擬的
bustle	[ˋbʌs!]	n., v.	喧囂
fabric	[ˋfæbrɪk]	n.	布料
headset	[ˋhɛd͵sɛt]	n.	耳麥
mount	[maʊnt]	v.	架置
display	[dɪˋsple]	n., v.	陳列、顯示器
detect	[dɪˋtɛkt]	v.	察覺、偵測
heartbeat	[ˋhɑrt͵bit]	n.	心跳
monitor	[ˋmɑnətɚ]	v.	監視
gear	[gɪr]	n.	器具
track	[træk]	n., v.	追蹤
latency	[ˋletnsɪ]	n.	潛伏
simulate	[ˋsɪmjə͵let]	v.	模擬
simulator	[ˋsɪmjə͵letɚ]	n.	模擬裝置
simulation	[͵sɪmjəˋleʃən]	n.	模擬
refresh	[rɪˋfrɛʃ]	v.	更新

口譯專業字彙 進階字彙

字彙	音標	詞性	中譯
fabricate	[ˋfæbrɪˏket]	*adj.*	組裝
infotainment	[ˏɪnfəˋtenmənt]	*n.*	資訊娛樂化
haptic	[ˋhæpˏtɪk]	*adj.*	觸覺的
oculus	[ˋɑkjʊləs]	*n.*	眼睛
exoskeleton	[ˏɛksoˋskɛlətn]	*n.*	外骨骼
capacitor	[kəˋpæsətɚ]	*n.*	電容器
artificial	[ˏɑrtəˋfɪʃəl]	*adj.*	人工的
biofeedback	[ˏbaɪoˋfidbæk]	*n.*	生物回饋技術
aesthetics	[ɛsˋθɛtɪks]	*n.*	美學
unobtrusive	[ˏʌnəbˋtrusɪv]	*adj.*	不唐突的
algorithm	[ˋælgəˏrɪðm]	*n.*	演算法
analytics	[ˏæn!ˋɪtɪks]	*n.*	解析學
encryption	[ɛnˋkrɪpʃən]	*n.*	編碼
ingenuity	[ˏɪndʒəˋnuətɪ]	*n.*	精巧的裝置、獨創性
programmable	[ˋprogræməb!]	*adj.*	可程式化的
embedded	[ɪmˋbɛdɪd]	*adj.*	嵌入的

A reporter from Best TV is covering the Wearable Device & Technology Expo in Tokyo.

倍斯特電視台的記者正在東京進行國際穿戴式裝置科技展的報導。

Good morning, I'm reporting live from Tokyo Big Sight. The Wearable Device & Technology Expo just kicked off this morning, and from the crowd and bustle around me, our viewers might have a feel of the vibrant atmosphere.

早安,記者在東京有明國際展覽館現場報導。國際穿戴式裝置科技展今天早上才剛開始,從我周圍的群眾和喧囂,觀眾可能感受到很活躍的氣氛。

This year there are 260 exhibitors from 32 countries. Japanese exhibitors take up the largest number of booths, followed by Taiwanese exhibitors.

今年有來自 32 個國家的 260 家參展廠商。日本的參展廠商攤位是最多的,其次是來自台灣的參展廠商。

The most common devices include smart glasses, smart watches, and smart fabrics. Wearable healthcare devices,

最普遍的裝置有智慧型眼鏡、手錶及紡織品。穿戴式健康照護裝置,例如助聽器、心跳監測

such as hearing aids, heartbeat monitors, and powered exoskeletons, have gained more market share in the past few years and are also a major appeal in this expo.

器和動力外骨骼，在過去幾年市佔率不斷增加，也是這次展覽的主要吸引力。

Another exciting area is the AR/VR sector, which showcases AR/VR Apps, related systems, and hoad mounted display.

另一個讓人興奮的區域是 AR/VR 區，這裡展示了 AR/VR App、相關系統及頭戴式顯示器。

設計類
1

建築類
2

醫療器材、科技類
3

飯店、餐飲類
4

國貿類
5

203

❶ The IoT zone caters to the needs of IT professionals.

❷ 10 manufacturers from Taiwan participated in this expo.

❸ VR technology can be utilized in entertainment, education, and medical fields.

❹ Head mounted displays might be applied to extreme sports.

❺ Some smart watches can monitor heartbeats and blood pressure.

❻ The number of wearable device sales in Asia surpassed that in North America in 2014.

❼ Visitors can experience VR technology in this sector.

❽ In aging societies, the sales of wearable healthcare devices have kept rising.

① 物聯網區迎合了 IT 專業人士的需求。

② 來自台灣的十家製造商參加了這次展覽。

③ VR 科技能被使用在娛樂、教育及醫療領域。

④ 頭戴式顯示器可能被應用在極限運動。

⑤ 某些智慧型手表能監測心跳及血壓。

⑥ 在 2014，亞洲的穿戴式裝置銷售數量超越了北美洲。

⑦ 訪客能在這一區體驗 VR 科技。

⑧ 在人口老化的社會，穿戴式健康照護裝置的銷售量持續上升。

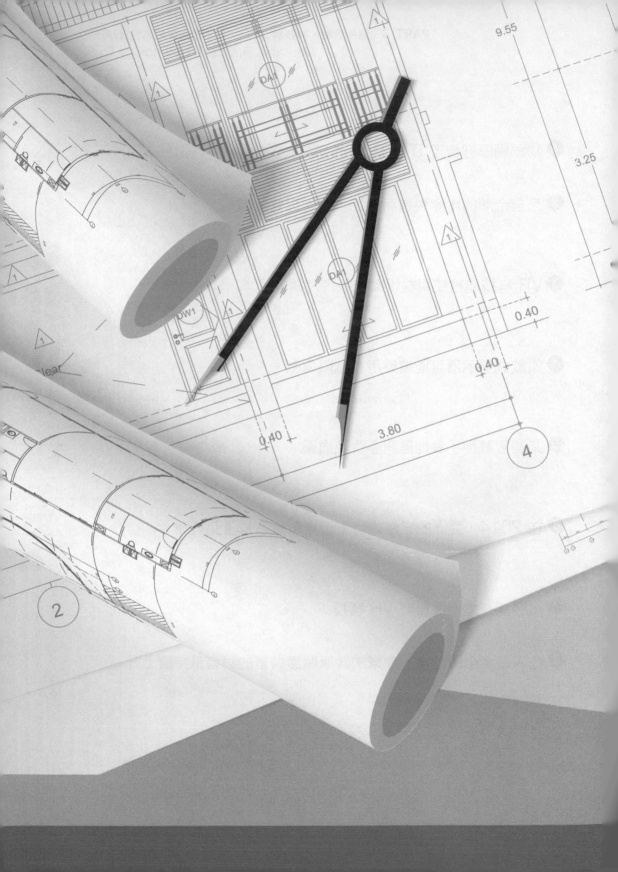

PART 4

飯店、餐飲類

篇章概述

飯店和餐飲類的口譯較容易上手，當中涉及的字彙多為求學中就學過的字彙。篇章中能擴充應用的層面很廣，包含短演講、課程介紹、舉辦記者會、司儀介紹開幕典禮、介紹產品特色等等，好好練習絕對能大幅增進口譯跟求職力。

32

飯店、餐飲展

國際飯店展
International Hotel Show

口譯專業字彙 基礎字彙

字彙	音標	詞性	中譯
fluctuation	[ˌflʌktʃʊˈeʃən]	n.	波動
hospitality	[ˌhɑspɪˈtælətɪ]	n.	招待
unaffected	[ˌʌnəˈfɛktɪd]	adj.	不受影響的
prosper	[ˈprɑspɚ]	v.	繁榮
venue	[ˈvɛnju]	n.	集會地點
array	[əˈre]	n.	一系列
catering	[ˈketərɪŋ]	n.	外燴服務
culinary	[ˈkjulɪˌnɛrɪ]	adj.	烹飪的
consumerism	[kənˈsjumərɪzm]	n.	消費主義
impart	[ɪmˈpɑrt]	v.	傳授
profitable	[ˈprɑfɪtəb!]	adj.	有利的
branch out	[bræntʃ aʊt]	v. phr.	擴展
abundant	[əˈbʌndənt]	adj.	豐富的
hotelier	[ˌhotɛˈlɪr]	n.	旅館經營者
diversified	[daɪˈvɚsəˌfaɪd]	adj.	多樣化的
pavilion	[pəˈvɪljən]	n.	展示館

口譯專業字彙　　進階字彙

字彙	音標	詞性	中譯
amenity	[əˋmɛnətɪ]	n.	便利設施
complimentary	[ˌkɑmpləˋmɛntərɪ]	adj.	贈送的
reception	[rɪˋsɛpʃən]	n.	接待處
concierge	[ˌkɑnsɪˋɛrʒ]	n.	櫃檯服務員
junket	[ˋdʒʌŋkɪt]	n.	公費旅遊
convention	[kənˋvɛnʃən]	n.	大會
suite	[swit]	n.	套房
voucher	[ˋvaʊtʃɚ]	n.	票券
valet	[ˋvælɪt]	n.	清洗衣物 或代客泊車的服務員
excursion	[ɪkˋskɝʒən]	n.	短程旅行、遊覽團
invoice	[ˋɪnvɔɪs]	n.	發票、發貨單
refurbishment	[rɪˋfɝbɪʃmənt]	n.	整修
corkage	[ˋkɔrkɪdʒ]	n.	開瓶費
bellboy	[ˋbɛlˌbɔɪ]	n.	行李員
franchise	[ˋfrænˌtʃaɪz]	v., n.	經銷權
franchisee	[ˌfræntʃaɪˋzi]	n.	特許經營者，加盟者

設計類 1
建築類 2
醫療器材、科技類 3
飯店、餐飲類 4
國貿類 5

The curator of the International Hotel Show is giving a brief speech in the opening ceremony.

國際飯店展的策展人正在開幕典禮進行一場簡短演講。

Despite the fluctuations in global economy in the past decade, the hospitality industry has not only remained unaffected, but also kept prospering, indicated by the 8% increase in our exhibitors.

儘管過去十年全球經濟波動，旅遊餐飲業不但沒受到影響，仍持續繁榮，由我們的參展廠商增加 8%可以顯示。

Our show offers a venue for hospitality professionals to attain the most updated information from an array of sectors efficiently.

我們的展覽提供一個讓旅遊餐飲業專業人士能有效率地獲得各部門最新資訊的場合。

The show is composed of four pavilions, which are Future Trend, Catering and Culinary service, Consumerism in the Digital Era, and Advanced Training respectively.

這次展覽由四個展館組合成，分別是未來趨勢、外燴及餐飲服務、數位時代的消費主義及高階訓練。

In the conferences in the Future Trend pavilion, senior hotel executives and hospitality management professors will address the patterns for success in the ever-changing global market, while in Consumerism in the Digital Era, specialists will impart how hotel owners can utilize big data to make their businesses more profitable.

I would also like to point out that in the other two pavilions, professionals who wish to advance their careers and branch out their networks will find abundant information from the diversified exhibitors.

在未來趨勢館的會議中，高階飯店主管及旅遊餐飲管理系教授將針對在瞬息萬變的全球市場中取得成功的模式，發表看法。而在數位時代的消費主義展館，專家將傳授旅館業者如何利用大數據增加企業獲利。

我也想指出在另外兩個展館，想在職業上晉升及擴充人脈的專業人士能從多樣化的參展廠商獲得豐富的資訊。

設計類

1

建築類

2

醫療器材、科技類

3

飯店、餐飲類

4

國貿類

5

❶ The Catering Equipment Show is concurrent with the Taiwan International Hotel Show this year.

❷ The Taiwan International Hotel Show has enormous appeal to international business owners in the relevant industry.

❸ The forms of lodging include not only villas and resorts, but also hostels, B&B and pensions.

❹ Utilizing big data analysis will help hoteliers to boost their profits.

❺ Students majoring in Hospitality Management will acquire the latest trends in this show.

❻ There are 520 booths in total in the 4-day International Hotel Utility Show.

❼ The theme of this new pavilion is the application of smart electronics on security

❽ The smart electronics on display consist of surveillance and POS systems.

❶ 今年的台灣國際飯店展同場展出餐飲設備用品展。

❷ 台灣國際飯店展對國際相關業者有極大的吸引力。

❸ 住宿型態不只包含別墅和渡假村,也有民宿、B&B 和膳宿公寓。

❹ 利用大數據分析將能協助旅館經營者增加獲利。

❺ 旅遊餐飲管理科系的學生透過這次展覽能瞭解最新趨勢。

❻ 為期四天的國際飯店用品展一共有 520 個攤位。

❼ 這個新展館的主題是智能電子產品的保全應用。

❽ 展出的智能電子產品包含監控系統及 POS 系統。

33

飯店、餐飲展

飯店管理科系招生介紹
Hospitality Management Program

口譯專業字彙　基礎字彙

字彙	音標	詞性	中譯
admission	[əd`mɪʃən]	n.	入學許可
requirement	[rɪ`kwaɪrmənt]	n.	要求
brochure	[bro`ʃʊr]	n.	小冊子
comprehensive	[ˌkɑmprɪ`hɛnsɪv]	adj.	全面的
essential	[ɪ`sɛnʃəl]	adj.	必要的
reserve	[rɪ`zɝv]	v.	預訂
reservation	[ˌrɛzɚ`veʃən]	n.	預訂
internship	[`ɪntɚn ʃɪp]	n.	實習職位
resort	[rɪ`zɔrt]	n.	渡假村
collaboration	[kəˌlæbə`reʃən]	n.	合作
placement	[`plesmənt]	n.	職位配置、學生分班
equivalent	[ɪ`kwɪvələnt]	adj.	相等的
submit	[səb`mɪt]	v.	提交
rate	[ret]	n.	比率
diploma	[dɪ`plomə]	n.	文憑
certificate	[sɚ`tɪfəkɪt]	n.	結業證書

口譯專業字彙　進階字彙

字彙	音標	詞性	中譯
elective	[ɪ`lɛktɪv]	*adj., n.*	選修的、選修課程
branding	[`brændɪŋ]	*n.*	品牌創建
delegate	[`dɛlə,get]	*v.*	委派
demographic	[,dɛmə`græfɪk]	*adj.*	人口統計學的
mediate	[`midɪ,et]	*v.*	調解
turnover	[`tɝn,ovɚ]	*n.*	營業額、人員流動率
affiliate	[ə`fɪlɪ,et]	*v.*	隸屬於
charter	[`tʃɯtɚ]	*v., n.*	包租
curriculum	[kə`rɪkjələm]	*n.*	全部課程
incentive	[ɪn`sɛntɪv]	*n.*	獎勵
accredited	[ə`krɛdɪtɪd]	*n.*	認證的
referral	[rɪ`fɝəl]	*n.*	會員結盟、轉介
liability	[,laɪə`bɪlətɪ]	*n.*	責任、傾向
lodging	[`lɑdʒɪŋ]	*n.*	寄宿
statistics	[stə`tɪstɪks]	*n.*	統計
accounting	[ə`kaʊntɪŋ]	*n.*	會計學

A representative from the Hospitality Management program of Best University is introducing the program and the admission requirement.

倍斯特大學飯店餐飲管理課程的代表正在介紹課程及入學要求。

Hello, I am honored to talk to you about our diploma program, and give you an overview of the admission requirement. Afterwards, there will be 30 minutes for questions, and further details regarding the application process can also be found in the brochures and on our website.

嗨，很榮幸能跟你們討論關於我們的文憑課程，並對入學要求做出簡短介紹。之後會有三十分鐘的提問時間，關於申請過程的更深入細節也可以在手冊和我們的網頁找到。

We offer comprehensive curriculum which equips our students with essential knowledge and skills to work in every level of the hotel industry, from front desk operation and guest relations to housekeeping

我們提供全面性的課程，讓學生獲得在餐飲旅遊業各個階層工作的必備知識和技能，如前檯作業、客戶聯繫、客房清理和人力資源。

and human resources.

Our students are required to complete internships in the third semester, and with our long-term collaboration with the tourism industry, our internship placement rate has reached 100% over the past decade.

學生必須在第三學期完成實習工作。以我們長期和觀光業合作的關係，我們的實習配對率在過去十年已達到100%。

As for the admission requirement, a high school diploma or equivalent certificate is essential. Applicants must hold a minimum of GPA 3.5.

至於入學要求，高中文憑或同等學歷證照是必要的。申請者的平均成績必須至少 3.5。

Non-native speakers of English are required to submit an IELTS report of minimum band 6.

母語非英語的申請者必須提交至少六級分的雅思成績單。

❶ The first-year courses focus on background knowledge and theories.

❷ Internships allow students to convert knowledge into hands-on applications.

❸ Our advanced courses cater to those students who wish to advance to managerial positions.

❹ Internship locations might be boutique hotels, resorts, luxury SPA parlors or restaurants.

❺ Internships are likely gateways to full-time positions.

❻ The courses in the first semester are composed mostly of prerequisites.

❼ Fluency in English communication and writing is a requirement.

❽ Having at least two foreign language proficiencies accelerates the promotion of hospitality industry professionals.

① 第一年的課程以背景知識和理論為主。

② 實習工作讓實習生能將知識轉換成實際運用。

③ 我們的高階課程針對的是想晉升到管理階層職位的學生。

④ 實習地點可能是精品旅館、渡假村、頂級 SPA 館或餐廳。

⑤ 實習生工作很可能是全職工作的跳板。

⑥ 第一學期的課程主要是先修課程。

⑦ 流利的英語溝通及書寫能力是必要條件。

⑧ 擁有至少兩種外文能力能加速旅遊餐飲業的專業人士升遷。

設計類

1

建築類

2

醫療器材、科技類

3

飯店、餐飲類

4

國貿類

5

34

國際烘培展
International Bakery Show

口譯專業字彙　基礎字彙

字彙	音標	詞性	中譯
anticipate	[æn`tɪsə‚pet]	v.	期望
triennial	[traɪ`ɛnɪəl]	adj.	三年一次的
announce	[ə`naʊns]	v.	宣布
announcement	[ə`naʊnsmənt]	n.	宣布
historic	[hɪs`tɔrɪk]	adj.	有歷史意義的
hands-on	[`hændz`ɑn]	adj.	實際動手做的
session	[`sɛʃən]	n.	講習會
artisan	[`ɑrtəzn]	n.	工匠、達人
ingredient	[ɪn`gridɪənt]	n.	原料
pastry	[`pestrɪ]	n.	酥皮點心
confectionery	[kən`fɛkʃən‚ɛrɪ]	n.	甜食
acclaimed	[ə`klemd]	adj.	受到讚揚的
logistics	[lo`dʒɪstɪks]	n.	物流
sector	[`sɛktə]	n.	部分、部門
facet	[`fæsɪt]	n.	方面
chef	[ʃɛf]	n.	主廚

口譯專業字彙　進階字彙

字彙	音標	詞性	中譯
sugarcraft	[ˈʃʊgɚ͵kræft]	n.	塑糖工藝
fondant	[ˈfɑndənt]	n.	翻糖
piping	[ˈpaɪpɪŋ]	n.	（蛋糕的）花飾
culinary	[ˈkjulɪ͵nɛrɪ]	adj.	烹飪的
extruder	[ɛkˈstrud]	v.	擠出
extruder	[ɛkˈstrudɚ]	n.	擠壓機
icing	[ˈaɪsɪŋ]	n.	糖衣
frosting	[ˈfrɔstɪŋ]	n.	糖霜
curdle	[ˈkɝd!]	v.	凝結
dredge	[drɛdʒ]	v.	撒粉
sieve	[sɪv]	n., v.	篩、篩子
knead	[nid]	v.	揉捏
dough	[do]	n.	麵糰
spatula	[ˈspætjələ]	n.	抹刀
colander	[ˈkʌləndɚ]	n.	濾盆
grater	[ˈgretɚ]	n.	磨碎器

設計類 1

建築類 2

科技類 醫療器材、 3

餐飲類 飯店、 4

國貿類 5

A press conference on the International Bakery Show is being held.

Welcome to the highly-anticipated triennial bakery show. This year we are proud to announce that the number of our exhibitors has reached a historic high, with 665 exhibitors from 52 countries. Another exciting announcement is the new educational section, where artisan bakers will present the latest baking techniques, and hands-on sessions will be provided. Take cake decorating techniques for example, they feature sugarcraft, fondant, piping, and creating 3D characters.

This show covers all sectors of

一場國際烘培展的記者會正在舉辦。

歡迎來到眾所期待，三年一度的烘培展。今年我們很驕傲地宣布參展廠商數量達到歷史新高，有來自 52 個國家共 665 家參展廠商。另外一個讓人興奮的消息是新的教育區，在教育區烘培大師將示範最新烘培技術，也將提供實際動手操作的研習課。以蛋糕裝飾技術為例，焦點有塑糖工藝、翻糖、花飾及 3D 角色製作。

這次展覽涵蓋了烘培產

the bakery industry, from ingredients, pastry, and confectionery to baking and packaging equipment.

業的所有部門，包括原料、酥皮點心、甜食及烘培和包裝設備。

Also highly acclaimed is the logistics sector, in which visitors will be informed about how to manage raw materials, products, packaging, storage and shipping, etc. in the intricate logistics system.

另一備受讚賞的部門是物流部門，訪客能在這個部門將能得知在複雜的物流系統中，如何管理原料、產品、包裝、儲存和出貨等資訊。

Since the comprehensive show connects all the facets of this industry, chefs and bakery owners will not only gain access to a variety of suppliers and equipment manufacturers, but also broaden their consumer base efficiently.

因為這場全面性的展覽串連了這產業的所有面向，主廚和烘培坊業者不但能接觸到多樣化的供應商和設備製造商，也能有效率地擴大他們的消費者群。

設計類

1

建築類

2

醫療器材、科技類

3

飯店、餐飲類

4

國貿類

5

❶ The sector covers baking tools and pastry ingredients.

❷ Professional pastry chefs will demonstrate intricate techniques.

❸ Sugarcraft and fondant have become the most popular cake decorating techniques.

❹ This bakery show offers the largest B2B trade platform in the related industry in Asia.

❺ The integrated bakery show encompasses a wide spectrum of sectors.

❻ The topics of the speeches range from marketing to logistics.

❼ It is quite an eye-opener to attend the seminar on the latest trend of baking.

❽ The show gathers bakery owners, food manufacturers, and bakery institutions.

❶ 這個部門涵蓋烘培工具和西點原料。

❷ 專業西點主廚將示範複雜的技巧。

❸ 塑糖工藝和翻糖已經變成最受歡迎的蛋糕裝飾技巧。

❹ 這場烘培展提供亞洲相關產業中最大的 B2B 貿易平台

❺ 這場複合式的烘培展涵蓋多樣化的部門。

❻ 演講的主題有行銷及行銷物流系統。

❼ 參加最新烘培趨勢的研習會真是令人大開眼界。

❽ 這場展覽集結了烘培坊業主、食品製造商和烘培訓練機構。

設計類 1

建築類 2

醫療器材、科技類 3

飯店、餐飲類 4

國貿類 5

35

飯店、餐飲展

台北國際茶與咖啡展
Taipei International Tea and Coffee Show

口譯專業字彙　基礎字彙

字彙	音標	詞性	中譯
ancillary	[`ænsə͵lɛrɪ]	adj.	輔助的
concurrent	[kənˋkɚrənt]	adj.	同時發生的
barista	[bɑˋrɪstə]	n.	咖啡師
latte art	[ˊlɑ͵tɛ ɑrt]	n.	拉花藝術
encompass	[ɪnˋkʌmpəs]	v.	包含
refreshment	[rɪˋfrɛʃmənt]	n.	茶點
prime	[praɪm]	adj.	主要的
presence	[ˋprɛzns]	n.	存在、能見度
expand	[ɪkˋspænd]	v.	擴充
coverage	[ˋkʌvərɪdʒ]	n.	新聞報導
significant	[sɪgˋnɪfəkənt]	adj.	重要的
raw	[rɔ]	adj.	生的、未加工的
panel	[ˋpæn!]	n.	評審小組
savor	[ˋsevɚ]	v.	品嚐
competitor	[kəmˋpɛtətɚ]	n.	競爭者
judge	[dʒʌdʒ]	n.	裁判

口譯專業字彙　進階字彙

字彙	音標	詞性	中譯
cupping	[ˋkʌpɪŋ]	n.	咖啡杯測
mocha	[ˋmokə]	n.	摩卡
cappuccino	[ˌkapəˋtʃino]	n.	卡布奇諾
espresso	[ɛsˋprɛso]	n.	濃縮咖啡
doppio	[ˋdɑpɪo]	n.	雙倍濃縮咖啡
macchiato	[ˌmɑkɪˋɑto]	n.	瑪奇朵咖啡
bland	[blænd]	adj.	無刺激性的
brew	[bru]	v.	釀造、泡茶、煮咖啡
filtration	[fɪlˋtreʃən]	n.	過濾
frother	[frɑθɚ]	n.	起泡器
decaffeinated	[diˋkæfɪˌnetɪd]	adj.	去除咖啡因的
filter	[ˋfɪltɚ]	n.	濾器
roast	[rost]	v.	烘烤
aroma	[əˋromə]	n.	香氣
tamper	[ˋtæmpɚ]	n.	搗棒
fermentation	[ˌfɝmɛnˋteʃən]	n.	發酵

The emcee in the opening ceremony of Taipei International Tea and Coffee Show is giving a short introduction.

台北國際茶與咖啡展開幕典禮的司儀正在進行一段簡短的介紹。

It is my honor to present the highlights of the show to you. The 4-day show is a one-stop venue for buyers and suppliers in various facets of the tea and coffee business.

很榮幸像你們呈現這次展覽的重點。對茶與咖啡業各界的買家和供應商而言，為期四天的展覽是一站式服務的集會地點。

With 165 exhibitors and 285 booths, the show offers a prime opportunity to build brand presence, expand media coverage and create significant sales.

這次有 165 家參展廠商和 285 個攤位，提供了建立品牌能見度、增加媒體報導和創造重要業績的絕佳的機會。

The show encompasses five categories: raw materials, processed tea and coffee products, refreshments, ancillary

這次展覽包含五個類別：原料、茶與咖啡加工產品、茶點、輔助設備及咖啡師訓練課程。

equipment and barista training. Also, two concurrent events are the Taiwan Barista Championship and Taiwan Latte Art Championship. Competitors will prepare several specialty drinks and demonstrate their latte art skills to a panel of international judges.

Let's not forget that Taiwan is renowned for its tea culture. If you are not familiar with the local tea culture, please make sure to savor the unique tea products in the Taiwanese exhibitors' booths, such as High Mountain Oolong, Longjing Green Tea, and Sun Moon Lake black tea.

另外，兩場同時舉辦的活動是台灣咖啡師冠軍賽和台灣拉花冠軍賽，參賽者將製作數杯特色咖啡，並向國際評審小組展現拉花藝術。

別忘了台灣以茶葉文化知名。如果你不熟悉台灣本土的茶葉文化，請務必在台灣參展廠商的攤位品嘗獨特的茶類產品，例如高山烏龍、龍井綠茶和日月潭紅茶。

設計類
1
建築類
2
醫療器材、科技類
3
飯店、餐飲類
4
國貿類
5

❶ In this Barista Championship Competition, competitors have only 15 minutes to prepare four espressos and four macchiatos.

❷ Competitors display their techniques and creativity in this Latte Art Competition.

❸ Mr. Wu from Taiwan was named the World Barista Champion in 2016.

❹ Competitors' performance is evaluated by the taste of beverage and creativity.

❺ The coffee seminar educates the attendees on brewing techniques.

❻ Tea leaves are increasingly used as a culinary ingredient.

❼ Taiwan is famous for processed tea products.

❽ These booths showcase creative beverages prepared by Taiwanese tea shops.

❶ 在這場咖啡師冠軍競賽，參賽者只有十五分鐘準備四杯濃縮咖啡及四杯瑪奇朵咖啡。

❷ 參賽者在拉花競賽展示他們的技巧及創意。

❸ 來自台灣的吳先生獲選為 2016 年的世界拉花藝術冠軍。

❹ 參賽者的表現是由飲料的味道及創意被評判。

❺ 這場咖啡研習會教導參與者關於煮咖啡的技巧。

❻ 茶葉漸漸被使用為烹飪的原料。

❼ 台灣以加工茶產品出名。

❽ 這些攤位展示台灣茶飲店製作的創意飲料。

36

飯店、餐飲展

香港飯店管理培訓 Hotel Training Program in Hong Kong

口譯專業字彙　基礎字彙

字彙	音標	詞性	中譯
illustrate	[`ɪləstret]	v.	說明
trainee	[tre`ni]	n.	受訓者
attendee	[ə`tɛndi]	n.	出席者
qualification	[ˌkwɑləfə`keʃən]	n.	資格
evaluation	[ɪˌvæljʊ`eʃən]	n.	評估
hands-on	[`hændz`ɑn]	adj.	實際操作的
immerse	[ɪ`mɝs]	v.	沉浸
fast-paced	[fæst pest]	adj.	步調快速的
invaluable	[ɪn`væljəb!]	adj.	非常寶貴的、無價的
workshop	[`wɝk`ʃɑp]	n.	工作坊、研討會
etiquette	[`ɛtɪkɛt]	n.	禮儀
participant	[pɑr`tɪsəpənt]	adj.	參與者
transition	[træn`zɪʃən]	n.	過渡
telecommunication	[ˌtɛlɪkəˌmjunə`keʃən]	n.	電信
switchboard	[`swɪtʃˌbord]	n.	電話總機
housekeeping	[`haʊsˌkipɪŋ]	n.	家務，打掃房間

口譯專業字彙　進階字彙

字彙	音標	詞性	中譯
occupancy	[`ɑkjəpənsɪ]	*n.*	住房
overbook	[͵ovəˋbʊk]	*v.*	超額訂房
overstay	[`ovəˋste]	*n.*	延期退房
lease	[lis]	*v., n.*	租賃
rollaway service	[`rolə͵we ˋsɝ-vɪs]	*n.*	加床服務
deposit	[dɪˋpɑzɪt]	*n.*	定金
profile	[`profaɪl]	*n.*	簡要介紹
portfolio	[pɔrtˋfolɪ͵o]	*n.*	文件夾、投資組合
registry	[`rɛdʒɪstrɪ]	*n.*	登記簿
interface	[`ɪntə͵fes]	*n.*	介面
interdepartmental	[`ɪntə͵dɪpɑrtˋmɛnt!]	*adj.*	各部門間的
segment	[`sɛgmənt]	*n.*	分段、部門
orientation	[͵orɪɛnˋteʃən]	*n.*	培訓、定向
litigious	[lɪˋtɪdʒɪəs]	*adj.*	訴訟的
clientele	[͵klaɪənˋtɛl]	*n.*	（總稱）顧客
managerial	[͵mænəˋdʒɪrɪəl]	*adj.*	管理方面的

設計類

1

建築類

2

科技類　醫療器材、

3

餐飲類　飯店、

4

國貿類

5

A representative from a 5-star hotel in Hong Kong is illustrating the training program.

一位來自香港五星級飯店的代表正在描述該飯店的培訓課程。

Our 8-month intensive training program is offered to university graduates who hold a degree in hospitality related major.

我們為期八個月的密集培訓課程是提供給旅遊餐飲業相關科系的畢業生。

The comprehensive program helps our participants to build their professional skills from the ground up, and after the completion of the program, participants will gain the qualification to enter our advanced management program based on individual evaluation.

這全面性的課程協助參與者從基層打底培養專業技能，完成課程後，依照個人評量，參與者能獲得進入高階管理課程的資格。

With hands-on training in most of our departments, from reception operation and housekeeping to customer and catering services,

透過在我們大部分部門的實際訓練，包含接待處運作、客房清理及顧客服務和餐飲服務，參

participants will become accustomed to the fast-paced workplace and gain invaluable experiences.

Moreover, the program offers workshops on customer service skills and international etiquette, as well as sessions on marketing and accounting, which will immensely benefit those who aim to advance to the management program.

與者將習慣步調快速的職場並獲得可貴的經驗。

此外，此課程提供客服技巧及國際禮儀的工作坊，和行銷及會計的短期研討會，對那些目標是進階到管理課程的學員將有極大的助益。

設計類

建築類

醫療器材、科技類

飯店、餐飲類

國賓類

① An orientation is held at the beginning of the training program

② All applicants must be bilingual and computer literate.

③ The training program is fortified by online classes.

④ Those who complete the training program will be qualified for managerial positions.

⑤ Hospitality industry professionals must demonstrate empathy while keeping customer relations.

⑥ Familiarity with international etiquette is necessary in order not to offend customers from various cultures.

⑦ One of the features of the training program is the leadership workshops.

⑧ The hotel franchise offers trainees opportunities to work in different countries.

① 這套培訓課程初期會舉辦新生訓練。

② 所有的申請者必須具備雙語能力及熟悉電腦操作。

③ 這套培訓課程透過網路課程加強。

④ 完成培訓課程的人將有資格晉升管理職位。

⑤ 維護顧客關係時，旅遊餐飲業的專業人士必須展現出同理心。

⑥ 熟悉國際禮節是必要的，以免冒犯到來自不同文化的顧客。

⑦ 培訓課程的特色之一是領袖能力工作坊。

⑧ 這間連鎖飯店業提供給受訓者到不同國家工作的機會。

37

飯店、餐飲展

台北國際食品展
Taipei International Food Show

口譯專業字彙　基礎字彙

字彙	音標	詞性	中譯
packaging	[`pækɪdʒɪŋ]	n.	包裝
status	[`stetəs]	n.	地位、情況
gourmet	[`gʊrme]	n.	美食家
cuisine	[kwɪ`zin]	n.	菜餚
gateway	[`get͵we]	n.	途徑
alliance	[ə`laɪəns]	n.	聯盟
wholesaler	[`hol͵selɚ]	n.	批發商
retailer	[`rɪtelɚ]	n.	零售商
garner	[`garnɚ]	v.	獲得
appeal	[ə`pil]	n.	吸引力
delicacy	[`dɛləkəsɪ]	n.	美味
platform	[`plæt͵fɔrm]	n.	平臺
produce	[`pradjus]	n.	農產品
poultry	[`poltrɪ]	n.	家禽
agriculture	[`ægrɪ͵kʌltʃɚ]	n.	農業
agricultural	[͵ægrɪ`kʌltʃərəl]	adj.	農業的

口譯專業字彙　進階字彙

字彙	音標	詞性	中譯
condiment	[ˋkɑndəmənt]	*n.*	調味品
Halal	[həˋlɑl]	*n.*	合乎伊斯蘭教律法的食物
gastronomic	[ˌgæstrəˋnɑmɪk]	*adj.*	美食的
delicatessen	[ˌdɛləkəˋtɛsn]	*n.*	熟食店
winery	[ˋwaɪnərɪ]	*n.*	釀酒廠
vineyard	[ˋvɪnjəd]	*n.*	葡萄園
vintner	[ˋvɪntnə]	*n.*	酒商
turnout	[ˋtɚnˌaʊt]	*n.*	產量
liquor	[ˋlɪkə]	*n.*	含酒精飲料
meat monger	[mit ˋmʌŋgə]	*n.*	肉商
disposal	[dɪˋspoz!]	*n.*	處置
sanitation	[ˌsænəˋteʃən]	*n.*	公共衛生
preserved	[prɪˋzɝvd]	*adj.*	醃漬的
sealed	[sild]	*adj.*	密封的
pallet	[ˋpælɪt]	*n.*	棧板
vegan	[ˋvɛgən]	*n.*	嚴格素食主義者

設計類 1

建築類 2

醫療器材、科技類 3

飯店、餐飲類 4

國貿類 5

A reporter from ABC channel is covering the main features of Taipei International Food Show.

Famous for its gastronomic culture, Taiwan has established its status as the hub of gourmet food in Asia, which is why the Taipei International Food Show offers the best gateway to enter the Asian market and expand your alliance with manufacturers, wholesalers, retailers, and distributors.

As usual, the major appeal is the array of categories, such as fresh produce, poultry, seafood, canned and frozen food, beverages, and confectionery.

Besides, several new components have been added to

一位 ABC 頻道的記者正在報導台北國際食品展的主要特色。

台灣以美食文化出名，並已建立它在亞洲身為美食集散地的地位。這就是為何台北國際食品展提供了進入亞洲市場的最佳途徑，及與製造商、批發商、零售商和經銷商結盟的豐富機會。

如同以往，主要的吸引力是多樣化的種類，例如未加工農產品、家禽、海鮮、罐頭及冷凍食品、飲料和糖果類。

此外，今年的展覽加入幾個新元素，包括清真

this year's show, including the Halal Food Section, Star Chef Demonstration, and New Trend Seminars.

認證的食品區，明星主廚示範和新潮流研討會。

It is worth mentioning that this year's show garners much more international attention, as the number of exhibitors is unprecedented, and so is the number of scheduled B2B meetings.

值得一提的是今年的展覽受到更多國際注目，因為參展廠商及預定 B2B 會議的數量達到前所未有的新高。

The exhibitors from Europe, the U.S., Australia and Asia compose a diversified platform.

廠商來自歐洲，美國，澳洲和亞洲，組合成多元化的平台。

❶ This pavilion centers on frozen processed food.

❷ International buyers are interested in the unique Taiwanese food.

❸ Many food shows have set up specific areas for Halal certified food.

❹ The hospitality industry in Asia have been trying to draw Muslim tourists.

❺ These food manufacturing factories are certified by HACCP or ISO.

❻ Sanitation maintenance equipment is on display concurrently.

❼ The food processing and pharmaceutical machinery made in Taiwan are highly recognized internationally for their stable qualities.

❽ Waste disposal is an important part in the restaurant business.

❶ 這個展館以冷凍調理食品為主。

❷ 外國買家對台灣特色食品感到興趣。

❸ 許多食品展已經設立專區展出清真認證的食品。

❹ 亞洲旅遊餐飲業近期嘗試吸引穆斯林觀光客。

❺ 這些食品製造工廠都通過 HACCP 或 ISO 認證。

❻ 同場展出衛生維護設備。

❼ 台灣製造的食品加工及製藥機械以穩定品質受到國際肯定。

❽ 廢棄物處理在餐飲業是重要的一環。

設計類

1

建築類

2

醫療器材、科技類

3

飯店、餐飲類

4

國貿類

5

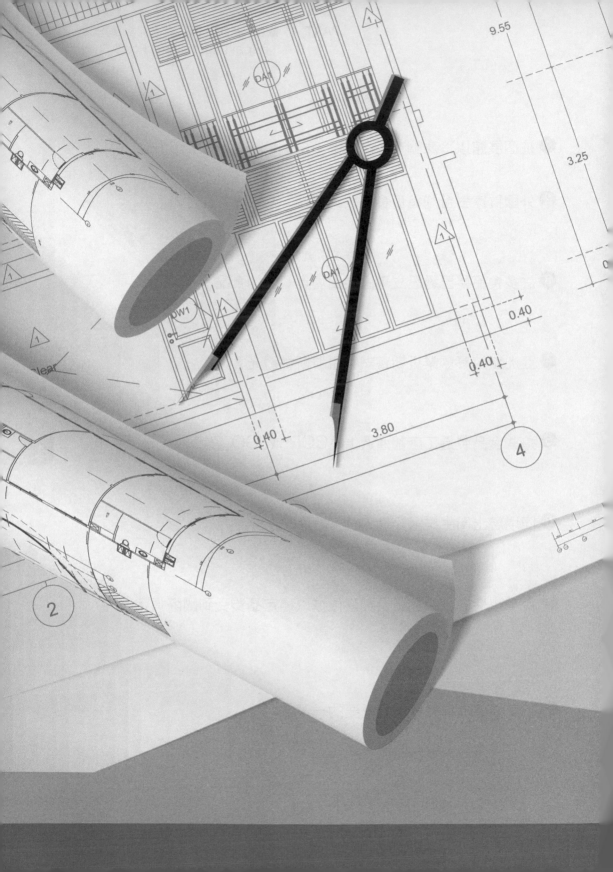

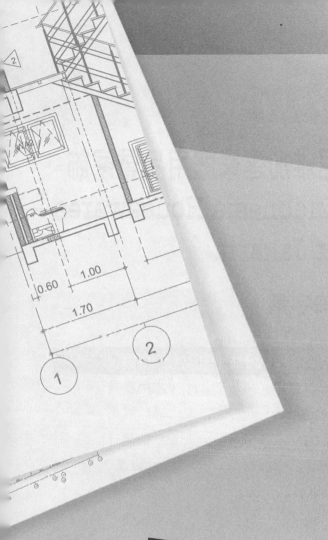

PART 5

國貿類

篇章概述

國貿類收錄的字彙對欲從事國貿業務人員來說都是個 bonus 喔，可以趁早學起來，在口譯或公司產品介紹時更無往不利喔。

38

國貿展

印尼雅加達家庭用品暨家飾展 Indonesia Housewares Fair Jakarta

口譯專業字彙　基礎字彙

字彙	音標	詞性	中譯
housewares	[`haʊsˌwɛrz]	n.	家用器具
glassware	[`glæsˌwɛr]	n.	玻璃器具
giftware	[`gɪftˌwɛr]	n.	禮品
textile	[`tɛkstaɪl]	n.	紡織品
decorative	[`dɛkərətɪv]	adj.	裝飾的
fortify	[`fɔrtəˌfaɪ]	v.	加強
strategy	[`strætədʒɪ]	n.	策略
tactics	[`tæktɪks]	n.	策略
urban	[`ɝbən]	adj.	都市的
urbanization	[ˌɝbənɪ`zeʃən]	n.	都市化
promising	[`prɑmɪsɪŋ]	adj.	有前途的
metropolis	[mə`trɑpḷɪs]	n.	大都會
metropolitan	[ˌmɛtrə`pɑlətn]	adj.	大都會的
furnishing	[`fɝnɪʃɪŋ]	n.	室內陳設
infuse	[ɪn`fjuz]	v.	注入、灌輸
lucrative	[`lukrətɪv]	adj.	獲利的

口譯專業字彙　進階字彙

字彙	音標	詞性	中譯
broker	[`brokɚ]	n.	掮客，股票經紀人
agent	[`edʒənt]	n.	代理商
supplier	[sə`plaɪɚ]	n.	供應商
authorize	[`ɔθəˏraɪz]	v.	授權
authorization	[ˏɔθərə`zeʃən]	n.	授權
dealer	[`dilɚ]	n.	經銷商
distributor	[dɪ`strɪbjətɚ]	n.	經銷商、分銷商
franchlser	[`fræntʃaɪzɚ]	n	授予特許經銷權者
importer	[ɪm`portɚ]	n.	進口商
exporter	[ɛks`portɚ]	n.	出口商
cargo	[`kɑrgo]	n.	貨物
shipment	[`ʃɪpmənt]	n.	運輸、貨物
yield	[jild]	n.	產量、利潤
revenue	[`rɛvəˏnju]	n.	收益
refurbish	[ri`fɝbɪʃ]	v.	翻新
stainless steel	[`stenlɪs stil]	n.	不鏽鋼

設計類

1

建築類

2

科技類 醫療器材、

3

嶺飲類 飯店、

4

國貿類

5

The curator of Housewares Fair Jakarta is outlining the highlights of the fair.

雅加達家庭用品暨家飾展的策展人正簡短描述這場展覽的重點。

Housewares Fair Jakarta is not only the one-stop fair for international manufacturers to enter the Indonesian market, but also the best gateway to the rest of the ASEAN countries.

雅加達家庭用品暨家飾展對各國製造商而言，不只是進入印尼市場的一站式展覽，也是打入其他東協國家的最佳途徑。

Visitors will be exposed to a spectrum of products, consisting of illuminations, glassware, porcelain, giftware, home textiles, decorative accessories, and kitchen appliances, etc.

訪客將能接觸到多樣化的產品，包括照明設備、玻璃器皿、瓷器、禮品、家用紡織品、飾品、廚房家電等等。

It is expected that 362 exhibitors from 58 nations and 450 buyers will participate in the fair.

預計有來自 58 個國家的 362 家廠商及 450 位買家參與這次展覽。

The uniqueness of the fair is

針對東協國家的行銷策

fortified by the keynote speeches on marketing strategies in the ASEAN nations and the latest trends of urbanization in Indonesia.

We are also delighted to unveil the first concurrent exhibition, the NEXT Interior Design and Furnishings Exhibition, where promising young designers from Indonesia and globally will display their creative designs that cater to the metropolitan lifestyle in Indonesia.

略和印尼都化會最新趨勢的演講，加強了這次展覽的特殊性。

我們也很高興宣布第一次的同場展覽，NEXT 室內設計和陳設展。來自印尼和全球的新銳年輕設計師將展出針對印尼都會化生活型態的創意設計。

設計類

1

建築類

2

科技類／醫療器材、

3

餐飲類／飯店、

4

國貿類

5

❶ The population in Indonesia is the largest among the ASEAN nations.

❷ The prosperous economy in Indonesia expands urban residents' need for housewares.

❸ This fair acts as a springboard for western manufacturers to branch out in the ASEAN market.

❹ The large population in Indonesia indicates a huge potential market for the housewares industry.

❺ These home decorations have an exotic style.

❻ Traditional Indonesian culture emphasizes family gatherings, which facilitates the growth of the home decoration industry.

❼ Emerging designers infuse new life into conventional home decorations.

❽ Our company is the authorized distributor of this brand.

❶ 印尼在東協國家中是人口最多的國家。

❷ 印尼的經濟繁榮擴大了都市居民對家庭用品的需求。

❸ 對西方製造商而言，這場展覽是在東協市場擴展的跳板。

❹ 印尼的大量人口意味著家庭用品產業的巨大潛在市場。

❺ 這些家飾品帶有異國情調的風格。

❻ 印尼傳統文化重視家族團聚，也促進家飾品產業的成長。

❼ 新銳設計師給尋常的家飾品注入了新的活力。

❽ 我們公司是這個品牌的授權經銷商。

39

國貿展

芝加哥家庭用品展 The International Home & Housewares Show Chicago

口譯專業字彙　基礎字彙

字彙	音標	詞性	中譯
cover	[`kʌvə]	v.	報導
accommodate	[ə`kamə͵det]	v.	容納
accommodation	[ə͵kamə`deʃən]	n.	適應、調解
variation	[͵vɛrɪ`eʃən]	n.	變化
various	[`vɛrɪəs]	adj.	各式各樣的
status	[`stetəs]	n.	地位、情況
aspiring	[ə`spaɪrɪŋ]	adj.	有抱負的
numerous	[`njumərəs]	adj.	眾多的
intelligence	[ɪn`tɛlədʒəns]	n.	智能
consult	[kən`sʌlt]	v.	諮商
consultant	[kən`sʌltənt]	n.	顧問
consultation	[͵kansəl`teʃən]	n.	諮詢
springboard	[`sprɪŋ͵bord]	n.	跳板
population	[͵papjə`leʃən]	n.	人口
exotic	[ɛg`zatɪk]	adj.	異國情調的
homeware	[`hom͵wɛr]	n.	居家用品

口譯專業字彙　進階字彙

字彙	音標	詞性	中譯
purchaser	[ˈpɝtʃəsɚ]	n.	採購人員
maneuver	[məˈnuvɚ]	n., v.	策略、巧妙地操縱
sanction	[ˈsæŋkʃən]	n., v.	認可、批准
unsanctioned	[ʌnˈsæŋkʃənd]	adj.	未批准的
renovate	[ˈrɛnəˌvet]	v.	翻新
tariff	[ˈtærɪf]	n.	關稅
duty	[ˈdjutɪ]	n.	關稅
stoneware	[ˈstonˌwɛr]	n.	石器
capital	[ˈkæpətḷ]	n.	資本、首都
legalize	[ˈligḷˌaɪz]	v.	合法化
licensed	[ˈlaɪsnst]	adj.	有許可證的; 有執照的
trademark	[ˈtredˌmark]	n., v.	商標、將…註冊為商標
copyright	[ˈkɑpɪˌraɪt]	n.	版權
patent	[ˈpætnt]	n., adj.	專利權、獲得專利的
intellectual	[ˌɪntḷˈɛktʃʊəl]	adj.	智力的
venture	[ˈvɛntʃɚ]	n., v.	冒險、投機

設計類

1

建築類

2

醫療器材、科技類

3

飯店、餐飲類

4

國貿類

5

A reporter from Best TV is covering the characteristics of the International Home & Housewares Show in Chicago.

來自倍斯特電視台的記者正在報導芝加哥家庭用品展的特色。

The International Home & Housewares Show in Chicago bridges top retailers and distributors in the U.S. with global buyers. On average, the show accommodated at least 2200 exhibitors and more than 60,000 visitors.

芝加哥家庭用品展將全球買家與美國頂級的零售商和經銷商聯結。平均來說，這場展覽容納至少 2200 家參展廠商及超過 60,000 訪客。

Often referred to as the largest trade show in the U.S., the show not only encompasses an array of household products, from decorations, lighting, and brewer accessories to healthcare and energy conservation products, but also has established its leadership status in household

這場展覽常被稱為美國最大的貿易展，不只居家產品包羅萬象，有家飾品、照明設備、釀造器具、健康照護及節能產品，也已經建立它在居家科技創新的領導地位。

technological innovations.

For instance, since 2016, the Smart Home Pavilion has been in the public eye, and showcased the latest technologies on how to transform an average home into an intelligent one.

例如，自從 2016，智慧屋展館一直受到大眾注目，展出如何將普通的家轉換為智慧屋的最新科技。

Also highly praised is the E-Marketing Center, where consultants who specialize in marketing strategies in the social media offer free consultations.

電子行銷中心也備受稱讚，這裡有社群媒體行銷專長的顧問提供免費諮詢。

Besides, the show offers a promising stage for aspiring young designers through the Student Designer Competition.

此外，透過學生設計競賽，展覽提供給有抱負的年輕設計師一個充滿前景的舞台。

設計類
1

建築類
2

醫療器材、科技類
3

飯店、餐飲類
4

國貿類
5

❶ You seem interested in the set of porcelain tableware.

❷ Would you like me to go over the features of these healthcare products?

❸ This is our catalogue with order information.

❹ Would you mind leaving some basic information?

❺ If you make a purchase directly at the booth today, you can have a 10% discount.

❻ Our company has established factories in China.

❼ We plan to increase our authorized dealers in the U.S.

❽ These energy conservation products are patented and protected by the intellectual property law.

❶ 您似乎對這組瓷器餐具感到興趣。

❷ 需要我幫您介紹這些健康照護產品的特色嗎？

❸ 這是我們的產品目錄，裡面有下訂資訊。

❹ 是否介意留下一些基本資料呢？

❺ 如果今天在攤位直接購買，可享有九折。

❻ 我們公司在中國有設廠。

❼ 我們計畫增加在美國的授權經銷商。

❽ 這些節能產品都有專利權並受到智慧財產權的保護。

設計類

1

建築類

2

科技類 醫療器材、

3

餐飲類 飯店、

4

國貿類

5

40

國貿展

英國國際禮品暨時尚生活用品展 Top Drawer London

口譯專業字彙 基礎字彙

字彙	音標	詞性	中譯
approve	[ə`pruv]	v.	贊成、同意
approval	[ə`pruv!]	n.	贊成、同意
organizer	[`ɔrgəˌnaɪzə]	n.	籌辦者
press	[prɛs]	v., n.	按壓、新聞界
conference	[`kɑnfərəns]	n.	會議
divide	[də`vaɪd]	v.	劃分
decade	[`dɛked]	n.	十年
handicraft	[`hændɪˌkræft]	n.	手工藝品
vibrant	[`vaɪbrənt]	adj.	活躍的
variety	[və`raɪətɪ]	n.	多樣化
exquisite	[`ɛkskwɪzɪt]	adj.	精緻的
selection	[sə`lɛkʃən]	n.	選擇
hail	[hel]	v.	為…喝采、肯定
range	[rendʒ]	n.	一系列
heirloom	[`ɛrˌlum]	n.	傳家寶
haute	[ot]	adj.	高級的

口譯專業字彙　進階字彙

字彙	音標	詞性	中譯
freight	[fret]	*n.*	運費、貨物
currency	[ˋkɝənsɪ]	*n.*	貨幣
conducive	[kənˋdjusɪv]	*adj.*	有益的、促成的
covenant	[ˋkʌvɪnənt]	*n.*	蓋印合同、契約
amalgamation	[ə͵mælgəˋmeʃən]	*n.*	合併
merger	[mɝdʒɚ]	*n.*	合併
symposium	[sɪmˋpozɪəm]	*n.*	研討會
conglomerate	[kənˋglɑmərɪt]	*n.*	企業集團
banner	[ˋbænɚ]	*n.*	橫幅
outsourcing	[ˋaʊt͵sɔrsɪŋ]	*n.*	外包
intermediator	[͵ɪntɚˋmidɪ͵etɚ]	*n.*	中間商
intermediary	[͵ɪntɚˋmidɪ͵ɛrɪ]	*adj.*	媒介的
indent	[ɪnˋdɛnt]	*n.*	委託採購
questionnaire	[͵kwɛstʃənˋɛr]	*n.*	問卷
confirmation	[͵kɑnfɚˋmeʃən]	*n.*	確認
compensation	[͵kɑmpənˋseʃən]	*n.*	補償

設計類 1
建築類 2
醫療器材、科技類 3
飯店、餐飲類 4
國貿類 5

The organizer of Top Drawer is addressing the features of this show in a press conference.

英國國際禮品暨時尚生活用品展的籌辦人員正在一場記者會發表這次展覽的特色。

Top Drawer is considered the largest gift show in the U.K. and a world-renowned trade show which drew on average 6300 local and international attendees each year in the past decade. The show is divided into 4 sectors, homeware, handicraft, fashion accessory, and gift.

英國國際禮品暨時尚生活用品展被視為英國最大的禮品展，也是世界知名的貿易展，過去十年平均每年吸引 6300 位本土和國際訪客。這場展覽區分為四個部分：居家用品、手工藝品、時尚配件和禮品。

Since the convention center is located in central London, designers, retailers, manufacturers and suppliers will immerse themselves in the latest trends embodied by a wide selection of exquisite brands.

因為會展中心位於倫敦市中心，設計師、零售商、製造商和供應商能沉浸在各種精緻品牌所展現的最新潮流中。

This year the show presents more than 1600 brands, many of which are hailed as trendsetters of avant-garde lifestyles.

In the handicraft and fashion accessory sectors, buyers will be delighted to find numerous high-quality products made of various materials, ranging from ceramic, porcelain, and glass to textile products.

The products showcased in the fashion accessory sector include haute handbags, heirloom-quality jewelry, watches and scarves, etc.

今年的展覽共有 1600 個品牌，其中許多被公認為前衛生活風格的潮流創造者。

在手工藝品及時尚配件區，買家會很高興找到許多各式材料製造的高品質產品，包含陶器、瓷器、玻璃及紡織產品。

時尚配件區的展品包括高級訂製手提包、傳家寶等級的珠寶、手錶、圍巾等等。

設計類
1

建築類
2

醫療器材、科技類
3

飯店、餐飲類
4

國貿類
5

❶ Would you mind filling out this questionnaire?

❷ Could you tell me a little about your company's background?

❸ Our company specializes in leather goods, such as wallets, handbags, and cellphone cases.

❹ The ex-work price is ten dollars per set.

❺ I am glad we can clinch the deal.

❻ Carrying out business in this vibrant metropolis is quite an eye opener.

❼ The stationery manufactured by our company occupied 10% of the market share last year.

❽ I'd like to know the volume discount you offer to retailers.

❶ 是否介意填寫這份問卷呢？

❷ 可以告訴我一些關於你們公司的背景嗎？

❸ 我們公司專營皮件，例如皮夾、手提包和手機套。

❹ 出廠價（ex-work price）是一組十美金。

❺ 很高興我們能完成這筆交易。

❻ 在這活躍的大都會進行商務令人大開眼界。

❼ 我們公司生產的文具佔了 10%市占率。

❽ 我想知道你們提供給零售商的總額折扣（volume discount）。

41 國貿展

東京國際春季禮品展
Tokyo International Gift Show Spring

口譯專業字彙　基礎字彙

字彙	音標	詞性	中譯
commence	[kə`mɛns]	v.	開始
gratitude	[`grætə‚tjud]	n.	感謝
staffer	[`stæfɚ]	n.	職員
represent	[‚rɛprɪ`zɛnt]	v.	代表
echo	[`ɛko]	v., n.	反應、呼應
revival	[rɪ`vaɪv!]	n.	復甦
festive	[`fɛstɪv]	adj.	節慶的
vivacious	[vaɪ`veʃəs]	adj.	活潑的
ambience	[`æmbɪəns]	n.	氛圍
exemplify	[ɪg`zɛmplə‚faɪ]	v.	例示
behalf	[bɪ`hæf]	n.	代表
delighted	[dɪ`laɪtɪd]	adj.	高興的
endow	[ɪn`daʊ]	v.	捐贈、賦予
stationery	[`steʃən‚ɛrɪ]	n.	文具
emerging	[ɪ`mɝdʒɪŋ]	adj.	新興的
chic	[`ʃik]	adj.	時髦的

口譯專業字彙　進階字彙

字彙	音標	詞性	中譯
semiannual	[͵sɛmɪˋænjʊəl]	adj.	一年兩次的
ornament	[ˋɔrnəmənt]	n.	裝飾品
fiscal	[ˋfɪsk!]	adj.	財政的
legitimate	[lɪˋdʒɪtəmɪt]	adj.	合法的
illegitimate	[͵ɪlɪˋdʒɪtəmɪt]	adj.	不合法的
fragrance	[ˋfregrəns]	n.	香氣、香水
staple	[ˋstep!]	n.	主要商品
endorse	[ɪnˋdɔrs]	v.	支票背書、認可
endorsement	[ɪnˋdɔrsmənt]	n.	支票背書、認可
burgeoning	[ˋbɝdʒənɪŋ]	adj.	發展快速的
selective	[səˋlɛktɪv]	adj.	精挑細選的
bond	[band]	n.	債券
preponderance	[prɪˋpandərəns]	n.	優勢
opponent	[əˋponənt]	n.	對手
epicenter	[ˋɛpɪ͵sɛntɚ]	n.	集中點
commission	[kəˋmɪʃən]	n.	佣金

設計類

1

建築類

2

醫療器材、科技類

3

飯店、餐飲類

4

國貿類

5

A representative of exhibitors is giving an opening address.

一位參展廠商的代表正在進行開幕演講。

Good morning, welcome to Tokyo International Gift Show Spring. What a lovely day to commence the show.

早安，歡迎來到東京國際春季禮品展。今天開始這場展覽真是美好的一天。

On behalf of the exhibitors, I'd like to express deep gratitude to the organizer, sponsors and all the staffers for working zealously to ensure the smooth operation of this show.

謹代表參展廠商，我想向籌備單位，贊助商和工作人員表達感謝，他們熱誠地工作確保展覽能順利進行。

The theme of the show is "Design & Revival", echoing the vivacious and festive spring ambience and exemplified by carefully selected designer products. International visitors might be particularly interested in the Nippon craft sector, in which traditional

這次會展的主題是「設計與復興」，呼應了活潑和歡慶的春天氣氛，並由精選的設計師商品展現。國際訪客可能會對日本工藝區特別感到興趣，在這區傳統日本工藝品被新興藝術家賦

Japanese crafts are endowed with new designs by emerging artists.

予了新設計。

The other must-visit sectors are Home Decorative Goods and Chic Items. The former gathers ornaments for all areas of a household, including those for living rooms, dining rooms, bedrooms and gardens.

其他一定要造訪的有家飾區和時髦品商品區。前者涵蓋住宅內所有區域的家飾品，包含客廳、餐廳、臥房和花園。

The latter encompasses diversified products, such as fashion accessories, apparel, beauty care products, and smartphone accessories.

後者涵蓋多樣商品，例如時髦配件、服裝、美妝商品及智慧型手機配件。

設計類

1

建築類

2

醫療器材、科技類

3

飯店、餐飲類

4

國貿類

5

❶ This is my name card. Please let me know if you need any assistance.

❷ We are hoping to collaborate with more suppliers to expand our business in Asia.

❸ His sales commission is 10% of the retail price

❹ Our logistics network will ensure the most efficient delivery.

❺ I will send you the relevant follow-up information shortly.

❻ Have you got our giveaways?

❼ Our staple is the line of fragrance products.

❽ We noticed that more and more potential customers are from the Middle East.

❶ 這是我的名片，讓我知道您是否需要任何協助。

❷ 我們希望能與更多供應商合作拓展在亞洲的業務。

❸ 他的銷售佣金是零售價格的 10%。

❹ 我們的物流系統能確保最高效率的運送。

❺ 稍後我會寄給您相關的後續資訊。

❻ 您有拿到我們的免費贈品了嗎？

❼ 我們的主打是這一系列的香氛商品。

❽ 我們注意到越來越多潛在客戶來自中東地區。

42

國貿展

美國手工藝品展
The Craft & Hobby World Fair

口譯專業字彙　基礎字彙

字彙	音標	詞性	中譯
correspond	[ˌkɔrɪˋspand]	v.	符合、通信
craftsman	[ˋkræftsmən]	n.	工藝家
interact	[ˌɪntəˋrækt]	v.	互動
prominent	[ˋpramənənt]	adj.	卓越的
eminent	[ˋɛmənənt]	adj.	名聲顯赫的
accolade	[ˌækəˋled]	n.	盛讚
origami	[ˌɔrəˋgamɪ]	n.	摺紙藝術
blotters	[ˋblatə]	n.	記事簿
wrapper	[ˋræpə]	n.	包裝紙、封套
quilting	[ˋkwɪltɪŋ]	n.	縫被工藝
crochet	[kroˋʃe]	n.	鉤針編織
patchwork	[ˋpætʃˏwɜk]	n.	補綴品
unabated	[ˌʌnəˋbetɪd]	adj.	不減弱的
boom	[bum]	n.	繁榮
diversity	[daɪˋvɜsətɪ]	n.	多樣性
invite	[ɪnˋvaɪt]	v.	邀請

口譯專業字彙　進階字彙

字彙	音標	詞性	中譯
requisite	[ˋrɛkwəzɪt]	n., adj.	必要條件、必須的
upcycling	[ˈʌpˌsaɪ.klɪŋ]	n.	升級再造
exclusive	[ɪkˋsklusɪv]	adj.	獨家的
courier	[ˋkʊrɪɚ]	n.	快遞
pamphlet	[ˋpæmflɪt]	n.	小冊子
assortment	[əˋsɔrtmənt]	n.	分類
commodity	[kəˋmɑdətɪ]	n.	商品
inflation	[ɪnˋfleʃən]	n.	通貨膨脹
monetary	[ˋmʌnəˌtɛrɪ]	adj.	財政的、貨幣的
valid	[ˋvælɪd]	adj.	有效的、正當的
validate	[ˋvæləˌdet]	v.	使生效
correspondence	[ˌkɔrəˋspɑndəns]	n.	符合、通信
administrate	[ədˋmɪnəˌstret]	v.	管理
administration	[ədˌmɪnəˋstreʃən]	n.	管理、行政
allocate	[ˋæləˌket]	v.	分配
allocation	[ˌæləˋkeʃən]	n.	分派、分配額

The organizer of the Craft & Hobby World Fair is illustrating the highlights of the fair.

美國手工藝品展的籌備人員正在描述展覽的焦點。

The fair gathers designers, craftsmen, retailers, distributors, buyers and suppliers. Attendees will not only familiarize themselves with traditional American crafts, but also interact with the prominent craftsmen from around the globe.

這次展覽集結設計師，工藝師，零售商，經銷商，買家和供應商。與會者不但能熟悉美國傳統工藝品，也能和來自世界各地傑出的工藝師互動。

I'm pleased to announce a new sector, the upcycling sector, which is highly informative on sustainable lifestyle.

很高興宣佈一個新展區，升級再造區，這個展區提供永續生活型態的豐富資訊。

The fair has received accolades for diverse products in the paper and textile sectors, from origami paper, blotters, and wrappers to quilting, crochet, and patchwork,

此展覽以紙類區和紡織類區豐富的商品受到讚賞，這些商品有摺紙，記事簿，包裝紙，縫被工藝、鉤針編織及補綴

to name just a few.

藝品，而這只是稍微列舉。

Besides, the jewelry sector has seen unabated boom according to our statistics of visitors and orders.

此外，根據訪客和訂單的統計數字，珠寶區一直維持盛況。

Another new addition is the exhibitors from Japan, Korea, and Taiwan, as well as ASEAN nations. We feel honored to have invited eminent designers and craftsmen from the above countries to give speeches on their specialties.

另一個新加入的元素是來自日本、韓國和，台灣及東協國家的參展者，我們很榮幸能邀請到來自以上國家的傑出設計師和工藝家進行關於他們專長的演講。

設計類

1

建築類

2

醫療器材、科技類

3

飯店、餐飲類

4

國貿類

5

1 Some experts will demonstrate their techniques and offer hands-on sessions.

2 For self-employed craftsmen, one of the most important purposes of participating in exhibitions is to expand their accesses.

3 The smooth operation of the booth depends on the efficient allocation of tasks.

4 We'd like to act as the sole agent of this brand in Taiwan.

5 Some investors purchase handicrafts made of rare materials for the probable increment of value.

6 Craftsmen attend the fair also in the hope of gaining attention from connoisseurs.

7 The number of transactions of artists' requisite items has remained stable.

8 We need to confer the conditions of this contract.

❶ 有些專家會示範技巧並提供實際操作的研習會。

❷ 對獨立工作的工藝家而言，參展最重要的目的之一是擴充人脈。

❸ 攤位的順利運作依賴的是有效率的任務分派。

❹ 我們希望能成為這個品牌在台灣的獨家代理商。

❺ 有些投資者購買稀有材質製作的手工藝品是為了有可能增值。

❻ 工藝家參加這場展覽也是希望得到鑑賞家的注意。

❼ 藝術家工作的必需品交易數量一直維持穩定。

❽ 我們需要商議一下這份合約的條件。

43

國貿展

香港玩具展 Hong Kong Toys & Games Fair

口譯專業字彙　基礎字彙

字彙	音標	詞性	中譯
flagship	[`flæg ʃɪp]	n.	旗艦、頂級的
fidget	[`fɪdʒɪt]	n.	坐立不安、玩弄
hand spinner	[hænd `spɪnɚ]	n.	指尖陀螺
bearing	[`bɛrɪŋ]	n.	軸承
quadrangle	[`kwɑdræŋɡ!]	n.	四邊形
oval	[`ov!]	adj.	橢圓形的
aluminum	[ə`lumɪnəm]	n.	鋁
respectively	[rɪ`spɛktɪvlɪ]	adv.	分別地
stress-relieving	[strɛs rɪ`livɪŋ]	adj.	舒緩壓力的
variant	[`vɛrɪənt]	n.	變化
specify	[`spɛsə faɪ]	v.	指明
enquire	[ɪn`kwaɪr]	v.	詢問
inquiry	[ɪn`kwaɪrɪ]	n.	詢問
entertainment	[ɛntɚ`tenmənt]	n.	娛樂
recreation	[rɛkrɪ`eʃən]	n.	消遣
appointment	[ə`pɔɪntmənt]	n.	任命、正式約會

口譯專業字彙　進階字彙

字彙	音標	詞性	中譯
widget	[ˋwɪdʒɪt]	n.	小器件
resin	[ˋrɛzɪn]	n.	樹脂
stereolithography (SLA)	[ˌstɛrɪolɪˋθɑgrəfɪ]	n.	光固化成形法
apportion	[əˋporʃən]	n.	分配
confer	[kənˋfɝ]	v.	商議、授予
recruit	[rɪˋkrut]	v.	雇用、徵募
downsize	[ˋdaʊnˋsaɪz]	v.	縮小規模
vacancy	[ˋvekənsɪ]	n.	空額
increment	[ˋɪnkrəmənt]	n.	增量、增值
laborer	[ˋlebərɚ]	n.	勞工
perk	[pɝk]	n.	津貼
personnel	[ˌpɝsnˋɛl]	n.	人事
temp	[ˋtɛmp]	n.	臨時僱員
customize	[ˋkʌstəmˌaɪz]	v.	訂做
quotation	[kwoˋteʃən]	n.	報價單
feasibility	[ˌfizəˋbɪlətɪ]	n.	可行性

設計類
1
建築類
2
醫療器材、科技類
3
飯店、餐飲類
4
國貿類
5

A staffer at the booth of ABC Toy Company is talking to an interested visitor about the company's products.

一位 ABC 玩具公司攤位的職員正在對一位感興趣的訪客講解公司產品。

Hello, I see you are looking at our fidget toys. May I guide you through the types of these toys?

嗨，我注意到您正在看我們的舒壓玩具。我能向您介紹這些玩具的種類嗎？

Over here are our flagship products, hand spinners, which come in three shapes.

這邊有我們的主打商品，指尖陀螺。共有三種形狀。

The shape that is the most popular with beginners is the tri-spinner. This one I am holding is made of copper with ceramic center bearing.

最受初學者歡迎的是三角指尖陀螺。我手上這個是銅器製作，中間有陶製軸承。

Besides, we have quad spinners and oval spinners, made of stainless steel and aluminum

此外，我們有四方形和橢圓形的指尖陀螺，分別以不銹鋼和鋁製作。

respectively.

All of our hand spinners are CNC machined and manufactured with SLA and laser molding technologies.

所有的指尖陀螺都經過 CNC 加工，並以光固化成形法（SLA）及雷射鑄模科技製作。

The other toys that you might find interesting and stress-relieving are these fidget cubes.

其他您可能會覺得有趣而且紓壓的玩具有這些紓壓骰子。

These are six-sided with six variants. For instance, on this side, there is the button for those who enjoy clicking.

這些骰子的六面有六種不同形式。例如，這一面有按鈕，適合喜歡玩按壓的人。

設計類

1

建築類

2

科技類 醫療器材、

3

餐飲類 飯店、

4

國貿類

5

❶ If you wish to know more details, please refer to the catalogue for the specifications of our products.

❷ if you make a 5-item purchase directly from our booth, you will receive a 10% discount.

❸ It is said that fidget toys were invented to help children with hyperactive tendency.

❹ Fidget toys were first popularized in the U.S.

❺ Our company is the sole agent of this fidget toy brand in China.

❻ It would be more efficient if you can confirm the date of the appointment at the booth.

❼ The future trend of the toy industry lies in smart toys, those with A.I. configuration.

❽ The feasibility of the promotion activities at our booth must be carefully evaluated.

1 如果您想了解更多細節，請參考我們的目錄上商品的詳細規格。

2 如果您直接在攤位一次訂購五件，可享有九折。

3 據說紓壓玩具是發明來幫助有過動傾向的小孩。

4 紓壓玩具最早在美國開始流行。

5 我們公司是這個紓壓玩具在中國的獨家代理商。

6 如果你能在攤位確定約定日期會比較有效率。

7 玩具產業的未來趨勢在於智慧型玩具，就是有人工智慧配置的玩具。

8 我們攤位上促銷活動的可行性必須審慎評估。

44

國貿展

台北寵物用品展
Taipei Pets Show

口譯專業字彙 基礎字彙

字彙	音標	詞性	中譯
organic	[ɔr`gænɪk]	*adj.*	有機的
herb	[ɝb]	*n.*	草本植物
herbal	[`ɝb!]	*adj.*	草本的
shampoo	[ʃæm`pu]	*n.*	洗髮精
conditioner	[kən`dɪʃənɚ]	*n.*	潤絲精
irritation	[ˌɪrə`teʃən]	*n.*	發炎
groom	[grum]	*v.*	梳理
groomer	[grum ɚ]	*n.*	寵物美容師
specialize	[`spɛʃəlˌaɪz]	*v.*	專精於
packet	[`pækɪt]	*n.*	小包
spray	[spre]	*v., n.*	噴液
deodorant	[di`odərənt]	*n.*	止臭劑
formula	[`fɔrmjələ]	*n.*	配方
feline	[`filaɪn]	*adj.*	貓科的
canine	[`kenaɪn]	*adj.*	犬科的
alcohol	[`ælkəˌhɔl]	*n.*	酒精

口譯專業字彙　進階字彙

字彙	音標	詞性	中譯
unscented	[ʌnˈsɛntɪd]	adj.	無香味的
veterinarian	[ˌvɛtərəˈnɛrɪən]	n.	獸醫
prospectus	[prəˈspɛktəs]	n.	企業簡介
initiative	[ɪˈnɪʃətɪv]	adj., n.	初步的、倡議
collaborate	[kəˈlæbəˌret]	v.	合作
collaboration	[kəˌlæbəˈreʃən]	n.	合作
paraben	[ˈparəbɛn]	n.	對羥基苯甲酸酯
anti-fungal	[ˈænti ˈfʌŋgl]	adj.	抗黴的
anti-bacteria	[ˈænti bækˈtɪrɪə]	adj.	抗菌的
certification	[ˌsɝtɪfəˈkɛʃən]	n.	認證、稽核
confirm	[kənˈfɝm]	v.	確認
verify	[ˈvɛrəˌfaɪ]	v.	核對
verification	[ˌvɛrɪfɪˈkeʃən]	n.	核對
allergy	[ˈælədʒɪ]	n.	過敏症
allergic	[əˈlɝdʒɪk]	adj.	過敏的
consignment	[kənˈsaɪnmənt]	n.	委託銷售

A sales representative from Best Pet Grooming is talking to a visitor at his booth.

一位倍斯特寵物盥洗用品公司的業務代表正在和一位攤位訪客談話。

Hello, welcome to our booth. Have you heard about our new brand? We specialize in organic and herbal pet grooming products.

嗨，歡迎來到我們的攤位。您有聽過我們的新品牌嗎？我們專攻有機和草藥類寵物盥洗用品。

Let me give you our sample kit, which includes the tester packets of all our products.

請拿一份我們的樣品包，裡面有所有產品的試用包。

Other than shampoo and conditioner, we have dry clean spray and dry shampoo powder with deodorant formula.

除了洗髮精和潤絲精，我們也有止臭劑配方的乾洗澡噴霧和乾洗粉。

Our products are mainly divided into two categories to cater to your feline and canine

我們的產品主要分為兩類，針對貓和狗伴侶，而且產品都不含酒精和

companions, and they do not contain alcohol and paraben. Even if your fur kids have extra sensitive skin, our products won't cause any irritation.

For pets that might have skin infection, you can choose from our line of anti-bacteria or anti-fungal formula products, which are unscented and vet recommended.

The other scented shampoos and conditioners are made from natural herbs with international organic certifications.

防腐劑。就算你的毛小孩有特別敏感的皮膚，我們的產品都不會造成任何不適。

針對有皮膚感染的寵物，您可以從我們的抗菌或抗黴配方系列選擇，這系列的產品都沒添加香味，而且經獸醫推薦。

其他有香味的洗髮精和潤絲精是用天然草藥製造的，而且有國際有機認證。

設計類

1

建築類

2

醫療器材、科技類

3

飯店、餐飲類

4

國貿類

5

❶ As you can see on display and from the catalogue, we offer a wide range of grooming products.

❷ Attached with the catalogue is the complete price list.

❸ For an order of the minimum quantity of 100 items, we offer a 30% distributor discount.

❹ I look forward to our collaboration.

❺ Our company mainly retails pet carriers.

❻ Our online B2B dealings have hit an unprecedented high this quarter.

❼ I will e-mail you the quotation sheet instantly.

❽ Could you offer your FOB price?

設計類

1

建築類

2

醫療器材、
科技類

3

飯店、
餐飲類

4

國貿類

5

❶ 如同您從展示和目錄看到的，我們的盥洗產品非常多元化。

❷ 隨目錄附上的是完整的價格單。

❸ 一筆至少 100 品項的訂單，我們提供 30%的經銷商折扣。

❹ 我很期待我們的合作。

❺ 我們公司主要零售寵物外出提籠。

❻ 我們網路的 B2B 交易量這一季達到前所未有的高峰。

❼ 我會立即 e-mail 給您這筆報價單。

❽ 是否能提供離港價 (FOB price)？

職場英語系列 002

與國際接軌必備的 中英展場口譯（附 MP3）

作　　者	莊琬君
發 行 人	周瑞德
執行總監	齊心瑪
行銷經理	楊景輝
企劃編輯	陳韋佑
封面構成	高鍾琪

內頁構成	菩薩蠻數位文化有限公司
印　　製	大亞彩色印刷製版股份有限公司
初　　版	2017 年 8 月
定　　價	新台幣 399 元
出　　版	倍斯特出版事業有限公司
電　　話	(02) 2351-2007
傳　　真	(02) 2351-0887
地　　址	100 台北市中正區福州街 1 號 10 樓之 2
E - m a i l	best.books.service@gmail.com
網　　址	www.bestbookstw.com

港澳地區總經銷	泛華發行代理有限公司
地　　　　址	香港新界將軍澳工業邨駿昌街 7 號 2 樓
電　　　　話	(852) 2798-2323
傳　　　　真	(852) 2796-5471

國家圖書館出版品預行編目(CIP)資料

與國際接軌必備的中英展場口譯 / 莊琬
君著. -- 初版. -- 臺北市：倍斯特，
2017.08 面 ; 公分. --(職場英語系列；
2)ISBN 978-986-94428-8-6(平裝附光碟
片)1.商業英文 2.口譯

　　805.18　　　　　　　106010392